In The Arms Of A Gangster 2
(Beautiee's Biography)

In The Arms Of A Gangster 2 (Beautiee's Biography)

BY

TRACY WILSON

http://beautifulpublications.com

Published by
Beautiful Publications LLC
Stratford, CT 06614

PRINT ISBN: 978-1-7343352-4-8
EBOOK ISBN: 978-1-7343252-5-5

Printed in the United States of America

Dedication

This book is dedicated to my husband, Bazil J. Osgood. When I'm in your arms, I'm in my favorite place, I feel loved, I feel safe, and I feel protected. I love you Bazil.

Chapter 1

"Hey Smalls," Bazil smiled as he opened the door to let Smalls inside...

"It's not good..." Smalls said as he came inside and closed the door behind him...

"What's wrong?" Bazil asked as he pulled me close to him...

"We need to sit down..." Smalls said as we followed him into the living room. Smalls sat on the chair, we sat on the sofa, and then Smalls continued... "The Grand Jury found probable cause... they've issued an indictment...

"Don't worry Beautiee... I gotchu..." Bazil said as I started crying...

"There's more..." Smalls sighed...

"What's wrong?" Bazil asked...

"Beverly filed a motion to revoke bond... and the judge granted the motion..."

"Whhhyyyyy?" I cried...

"Because of me..." Bazil answered with tears in his eyes...

"Because you're charged with a double homicide and the attempted murder of your husband, the prosecutor believes you'll run..." Smalls continued...

"I'm not going anywhere!" I screamed...

"They know that – they just want to break you!" Smalls gritted as he slammed his fist on the end table...

"So I'm going back to jail..." I whispered...

"Yes Beautiee..." Bazil answered...

"For how long?" I asked.

"You'll be in jail until you go to trial... and during the trial..." Smalls sighed...

"This isn't right..." I cried...

"Bazil?"

"Yes Smalls?"

"Promise me you won't do anything stupid..."

"Get the fuck out..." Bazil said as he stood up...

"I'm sorry..." Smalls said as he stood up to leave...

"Wait a minute!" I yelled.

"Yes Beautiee?" Smalls asked as he turned to face me...

"What the fuck am I supposed to do now? Wait for them to knock on the door? Wait for them to arrest me at work? How much time do we have?" Smalls didn't answer right away. He just stood there looking at us for a few moments before Bazil spoke...

"She has to turn herself in doesn't she?"

2

"I'm afraid so…" Smalls answered with his head down…

"When?" I asked…

"Tomorrow morning…" Smalls answered as he headed towards the front door…

"Will you be there?" I asked as he opened the door to leave…

"I'll see you in the morning," Smalls answered as he closed the door behind him…

"Come here Beautiee…" Bazil said as he pulled me into a kiss… "Please don't cry…" he said as he began kissing my tears off my face to no avail…

"Hey Smalls…" Bazil said as he opened the door…"

"Hey Bazil…" Smalls sighed. "You ready Beautiee?"

"No…" I whispered as tears streamed down my face…

"Please don't go…" Bazil cried as he grabbed me and held on tight…

"I don't want to…" I cried…"but I have to…"

"You don't have to…" Bazil cried as he kissed me… "We can run… we can go anywhere you want… just don't leave me… please…"

"I want to…" I cried between kisses… "but I can't…"

"You promised me… you'd never leave me again…"

"I know... I'm sorry... my Thirst Quencher..." At this point, Smalls was crying too. In that moment – I wanted to run. I didn't want to leave his arms. I wanted Bazil to take me away from all of it... but I knew I couldn't do that either... "I'll make it up to you... when I come back..."

"You promise?"

"Yes... my Thirst Quencher... I promise..." Bazil let me go, but he continued crying as I walked over to Smalls...

"Let's go..." Smalls said with tears in his eyes. I opened the door without looking back because I knew if I did – I wouldn't go through with it. Smalls and I walked out the door and when Bazil closed the door behind us, he broke down crying hard. I started to turn around and run back to Bazil, but Smalls put his hand on my shoulder. We stood in the driveway for a few moments until I gathered myself, Smalls wiped his tears, we got in the car, and headed to the Bridgeport Correctional Center.

Chapter 2

"How many we got today?" She asked as Smalls took me inside...

"Ten..." somebody answered.

"Name?" she asked when I got to the window...

"Beautiee Osgood..." Smalls answered.

"Are you her attorney?"

"Yes I am."

"Fill out this form please – Beautiee – come with me..." she said as she came out from behind the window. I ran to Smalls and threw my arms around him...

"I know..." he whispered as he hugged me back... "I'll be back as soon as I can..." Smalls said as he let me go and I watched him leave...

"Let me give you a piece of advice – suck up those damn tears – weak Bitches don't make it in here," she said as she pulled me behind the door with the other inmates...

"Let me tell you something..." I said. She stopped abruptly, turned to face me, put her hands on her hips, and looked me up and down before she asked... "What – little girl?"

"I'm nobody's weak Bitch..." I said with a smile.

"Ooohhh... it's like that... okay... we'll see..." she laughed as she turned back around and I followed her to the back of the line with the other inmates... "Attention Ladies..." she said as she walked from the beginning of the line to the end of the line and back to the beginning... "My name is Gert – I'll be processing each of you. You'll take off your clothes, you'll squat, you'll cough, and then you'll be escorted to the shower. After you take a shower, you'll put on this jumpsuit and you'll be brought back here. You'll each receive an Inmate ID, an Inmate Number, and an Inmate Handbook – I suggest you take the time to read the manual so you know what's expected of you. We'll begin shortly..." she said as she walked away to speak to someone else... "That one at the end talkin' about she's nobody's weak Bitch – we'll see if she talks that same shit after she meets Ugly..." she laughed.

"Girl – you don't know who that is?"

"Should I?"

"That's Beautiee Osgood!"

"Yea – so what?"

"That's Bazil's wife!"

"Oh shit! The one that was charged with the attempted murder plus two other murders? That's her?"

"Yea – that's her!"

"Damn Veronica – why didn't you tell me?"

"I thought you knew – everybody else knows!"

"Shit – if she's in her for all that – Ugly might be in trouble..." she laughed as she headed back to the line... "Alright ladies – one at a time – don't be shy – we all got the same thing – does anybody need pads?"

"I do..." Someone said...

"Me too..." someone else said...

"Me too!" I said quickly. I didn't really need a pad – I just wanted to get off the line like the other ladies...

"Come with me y'all – Veronica – can you get them while I process these ladies?"

"Okay..." she said as she went to the line...

"This way ladies..." Gert said and we all followed. We were all escorted to a waiting room. I watched as the first inmate left and then the second. "Alright Beautiee – your turn... "Gert said as she took me to a room with a private shower... "Take off your clothes – put them in this bag – and put this pad on..." she said as she gave me the pad...

"Thanks – I don't need it..." I said as I stripped and put my things in the plastic bag..."

"You could'a stayed on the line with the other ladies..." she said as she pulled me towards the shower...

"I could've... but I didn't want to..." I smiled.

"This isn't a game..." Gert said, annoyed...

"Good – 'cause if this was a game – I'd forfeit…" I said.

"Squat and cough." I did as I was told and stood up. "Take a shower and put on this jumpsuit…" she said as she handed me the jumpsuit. I took the quickest shower I've ever taken, dried off, and put on the jumpsuit. "C'mon…" she said as she took me by the arm and escorted me back to where the other ladies were being processed. "Here's your Inmate ID, your Inmate Number, and your Inmate Handbook – read it or not – time to go to your cell…" she said as she took me by the arm again and brought me to my cell. On the way down, I saw other ladies in their cells. Some looked up at me, some didn't pay me any mind – but one in particular stared right through me…

"Oh great – just what I need – please leave me alone…" I sighed to myself as I waked past her…

"Here's your cell – the doors stay open for a while – the common area's over there – they'll be an announcement when it's light out – once they make that announcement, everyone is to return to their cell for the night – welcome to prison…" she said as she turned and walked off.

"Sigh… I might as well sit down and get comfortable…" I said as I sat on the hard bed, picked up the Inmate Handbook, and started reading…

"Why you bein' all anti-social?" she asked as she came into my cell…"

"Oh God… I knew it…" I thought to myself before I spoke… "I'm just tired… it's been that kinda day…"

"You have plenty of time to read that damn book – let's go…" she said as she tried to grab me…"

"Don't touch me!" I snapped as I pulled my arm away…

"I'll touch you if I want to… when I want to…" she said as she walked towards me, backing me into a corner. By this time, all the other inmates gathered outside my cell to watch what was about to go down…

"I said don't touch me…"

"Why not? Don't you like girls?" she said as she touched my cheek…

"Stop it!" I yelled as I pushed her into the wall…

"This is gonna be fun…" she said as she came towards me and tried to kiss me…"

"Oh hell no!" I yelled as I lunged at her, knocking her to the floor. I jumped down and commenced to stomping that ass… "Don't – you – ever – touch – me – again – with – your – Burly - lookin' – ass – do – you – understand – me?" I got up and stood there with my fists clenched, ready to beat her ass down if she tried to come at me again…

"Alright – damn!" she laughed as she got up off the floor and wiped the blood off her mouth...

"Hmmm... I guess she ain't nobody's weak Bitch..." Gert laughed to herself as she watched from the other side before she came over... "Okay – shows over – clear out..." Gert said as she shooed everyone away from my cell.

"Now...where was I..." I sighed as I picked up the Inmate Handbook and started reading. The first thing I noticed was the handbook was 42 pages. "Damn..." I said out loud... "Oh well – at least I won't be bored..." I said out loud as I read the mission statement:

The Bridgeport Correctional Center shall protect the public, protect staff and provide safe, secure and humane supervision of offenders with opportunities that support restitution and rehabilitation by providing meaningful programming designed to support successful community re-integration.

"Bullshit!" I flipped to the table of contents and scrolled down to Addressing Staff, Following Orders, Personal Conduct, and Personal Safety – page 6... "More Bullshit!" I said as I continued reading – especially when I got to Personal Conduct:

You are required to conduct yourself in a responsible manner. A. You are not permitted to engage in behavior that disrupts the order of the facility, threatens security, endangers the safety of any person or imperils state or personal property. B. You are not permitted to make sexually suggestive remarks or gestures to any person. C. You are not permitted to make excessive noise or to use profanity. "So what the fuck just happened to me then?" I shook my head and started reading the paragraph under Personal Safety:

If you believe that your safety is at risk, report your concerns to a staff member immediately. The Department of Correction and this facility are committed to ensuring your safety.

"Yea right – fuckin' staff stood right there and watched – only thing they were committed to was declaring a winner in the fight!" I snapped. I glanced at the Clothing/Accessory, Personal Hygiene, Housing Unit rules, Fire Safety, Movement and Corridor Regulations and stopped to read what was outlined under Dining Hall:

1. You will have five (5) minutes after chow call to leave the unit before you are late. Being late will cause you to miss chow.
2. Cutting in line is not permitted.

3. You are responsible for receiving a complete tray; only one (1) trip through the serving line is allowed.

4. You are required to sit in the seat next to the last occupied seat at each table. Skipping seats is not permitted.

5. No items may be taken into the dining hall except your own utensils; no items may be taken from the dining hall.

6. You must eat with your housing unit or work detail.

7. You will have twenty (20) minutes to eat your meal.

8. You must take your tray to the scullery after you finish your meal and scrape it into the proper container provided.

9. You must leave the dining hall after you finish eating and proceed to your housing unit or assigned area.

I started crying when I got to page 22 and read paragraph A. under the Mail Section:

You may correspond and receive an unlimited number of correspondence at your own expense. You may write to anyone except: a victim of any crime you have been convicted of or in which disposition is pending...

"Oh Bazil..." I cried. When I got to page 25 and read the paragraph under Initial Visit it made me feel even worse:

You may receive two (2) adult visitors from your immediate family pending completion of processing your visiting Application Form or for seventy-two (72) hours after admission. You may add your two immediate family members to your visiting list after intake by submitting a request to your counselor. A back ground check will be conducted and they must have the same last name as you.

"I can't even have visitors..." I cried. "Everyone in my immediate family is married – no one has the same name as me." I didn't feel any better reading the Immediate Family or the Expanded Family Section either – I couldn't see my husband, my parents lived down south, and we don't have children. I kept turning the pages until I turned to page 27 and read the paragraph under Section G. Privileged and Professional Visits:

Visits between an inmate and their attorney or other credential individual from the community such as law enforcement officials, community agencies and program, shall normally be accommodated during the following time periods; 8:15am to 10:15 am, 12:45pm to 2:15pm and 6:30

pm to 10:30pm. Attorneys do not need to pre-schedule. All other professional visits need to be pre-scheduled through the Counselor Supervisors Office. The visiting rooms for professionals will be assigned first come, first serve.

"Thank God I can see Smalls..." I kept turning the pages until I got to page 28 and read the paragraph under Section H. – Telephone Regulations:

1. Telephone calls are only permitted between 9:00 a.m. and 10:30 p.m. (9:00-10:30am; 12:00-2:30pm; 7:00-10:30pm)
2. Five (5) calls a day of 15 minute duration are authorized.
3. You are not permitted to make third party calls or calls to Department of Correction officials or to a victim of a crime you are charged.
4. Telephone calls are not permitted during facility lockdowns.

Once I read number 3, I started crying again. "Bazil..." I cried. I kept turning the pages until I got to page 29 and read the paragraph under Section 18. Court Trip:

A. You must wear your own clothing unless you have none, in which case you will wear the state-issue uniform.

B. By 4:00 a.m. of the day of court, you must have your personal property packed and your bed stripped. Take your property and your bedding, including towels, to the A&P Room. The facility is not responsible for any property you leave behind in your housing unit.

C. You are only permitted to take legal materials with you that pertain to the case at hand. These materials must be surrendered to the transporting staff during transit. The materials will be returned to you when you are in secure lock-up at the court and, on the return, when you are back in the facility.

D. You will be subject to the use of restraints in accordance with Department policy. (Reference: A.D. 6.4, Transportation of Inmates).

E. A court lunch will be provided.

F. You are not permitted to obtain or receive any item from any person while on a court trip.

I groaned out loud when I got to page 30 and read Section 19. Orientation:

The next business day after admission to this facility, you will be required to attend an orientation session. The purpose of these sessions is to inform you of how the facility works, what your obligations are, and what programs and services are available. Counselors will answer any questions you may have. If you refuse to attend orientation a Disciplinary Report will be given to you by your unit officer. Under normal circumstances you can expect to be housed in a designated orientation unit for at least seven (7) days after being admitted to this facility.

I kept turning the pages until I got to page 33 and started reading Section 4. Speedy Trial:

Speedy trial is a petition from an inmate to the court having jurisdiction to initiate proceedings to dispose untried charges. There are three types of speedy trials that affect inmates in custody; (1) an inmate in custody solely because of charges pending in this state (C.G.S. Sec. 54-82m); (2) an inmate under sentence with untried charges pending in this state (C.G.S. Sec. 54-82c); (3) an inmate under sentence with untried charges pending in another state (C.G.S. Sec. 54- 186, Article III). To apply for a speedy trial under C.G.S. Sec. 54-82m, contact your attorney or initiate pro se. For the other speedy trial motions contact your counselor.

"Hmmmmm... maybe I can get a speedy trial..." I said as I smiled. I lay down on that hard ass bunk, closed my eyes, and dreamed of Bazil.

Chapter 3

When I woke up the following morning, I went through the motions, not really speaking to anyone. As soon as I heard the call for chow, I headed straight for the dining hall, silently praying for coffee. "Thank you Lord," I said. I was relieved when I saw the coffee. I didn't mind waiting in line. When it was my turn, I got my tray, went to sit down, and, as luck would have it, the next available seat was next to Burly...

"Damn!" I said out loud as I remembered the rules: You are required to sit in the seat next to the last occupied seat at each table. Skipping seats is not permitted...

"Sup Beautiee..." she said as she touched my hair...

"Stop touching me!" I screamed...

"Do we have a problem here?" the Deputy Warden asked as he came over...

"No problem here – ain't that right Beautiee?" she said as she put her arm around me...

"Yes there's a fuckin' problem – I keep telling her stop touching me but this Burly Bitch doesn't understand English!" I said as I got up...

"Sit back down!" the Deputy Warden yelled...

"May I please sit somewhere else? I don't want her touching me!"

"Sit back down as you were instructed – you only have 20 minutes – and you..." he said, turning to Burly... "Keep your hands to yourself – got it?"

"Yes sir," she answered as I ate. "Ooohhh... I like what them lips do..." she slurred as soon as the Deputy Warden was outta sight...

"So does my husband..." I said before I started drinking my coffee...

"I got a nice dildo I could fuck you with..."

"Ain't happening..."

"I bet your lips suck a mean pussy..."

"You'll never know..." I said as I got up to take my tray to the scullery...

"We'll see about that..."

"In your dreams..." I said as I continued walking away... until she caught up to me with a few friends...

"Yo Beautiee – what's your fuckin' problem?" she asked as she got in front of me and pushed me..."

"See – there you go touching me again – I said don't fuckin' touch me!"

"Beautiee – have you read the Inmate Handbook?" the Deputy Warden asked as he came over to us...

"Yes I have..."

"Did you specifically read the section on personal conduct?"

"Yes I did..."

"Do you understand you are violating the personal code of conduct by using profanity?"

"I understand..." I sighed...

"Very well – come with me..." he said as he took me by the arm and out into the corridor... "Beautiee – listen to me..."

"Okay..."

"I need you to follow the rules to the letter – they know who you are – and they're just looking for an excuse to keep you in here..."

"Well – if that's the case – I already gave them one..."

"What happened?"

"That Burly Bitch came into my cell last night – I told her not to touch me – she tried to kiss me – and I stomped her ass!"

"Were there witnesses?"

"Yes – plenty!"

"Okay – we'll get her on violating the code of conduct for making sexually suggestive remarks and gestures towards you – but you have to stop using profanity – they'll use any little thing against you in here..."

"Shit!"

"Beautiee! What the fuck did I just say?"

"I'on know – what the fuck did you just say?" I laughed...

"I'll see you later..." he laughed as he went to get Burly...

"I got somethin' for you Beautiee..." I heard her say as he took her by the arm and down the corridor.

"Oh shit – Orientation!" I said out loud as I ran to keep from getting disciplinary action...

Smalls came to see me after orientation and I couldn't wait to be alone with him so we could talk. "How'd your first night go?" he asked.

"It was one of the worst nights of my life!"

"I'm sorry Beautiee. How'd you sleep?"

"I slept without my husband!" I snapped. "I need conjugal visits..."

"You've only been in here for one night..." Smalls laughed - but I was dead serious...

"I said I need conjugal visits!" I screamed in his face as I grabbed his jacket with both hands...

"Beautiee..." Smalls gritted between his teeth... "If you don't take your hands off me I'm about to forget who I'm talking too...

"I'm sorry..." I cried as I collapsed into his arms...

"It's okay... but I need you to hold it together... I gotchu... but you can't come at me like that..."

20

"I know... but I'm in trouble..."

"What happened?" Smalls asked as he sat down beside me...

"Can you get me conjugal visits? Please?" I asked, completely ignoring his question...

"If it were that easy Bazil would be here with you now..."

"So you can't?"

"This ain't like it is on TV Beautiee..." Smalls sighed...

"What do you mean?"

"Conjugal visits are only allowed in 4 states: California, Connecticut, New York, and Washington..."

"Thank God I'm in Connecticut..." I breathed...

"Conjugal visits were originally set up to preserve families... and you and Bazil don't have any children..."

"Oh my God..."

"You have to go on a waiting list..."

"What the hell?"

"You have to have impeccable prison behavior..."

"Oh damn... I'm fucked..."

"And... you have to be incarcerated for at least 90 days..."

"What the hell am I gonna do?"

"Beautiee – it's only 3 months..."

"I haven't slept alone since we've been married... I need my husband..." I whispered as I started crying again...

"Once you're approved, you can get visits from 24 hours to 3 days, once a month..."

"I hope I'm not in here too long..."

"Beautiee – I need you to listen to me..."

"Okay..."

"You'll be strip-searched and piss-tested going in... and coming out..."

"Oh my God..."

"Once you close the door behind you, you get interrupted..."

"Interrupted?"

"They call you to come out when they do their rounds... just like when you're in your cell..."

"What?"

"And you have to come out so they can see you..."

"Damn..."

"There's also a tower above you – and the tower officer verifies you've been accounted for – and if you're on medication, they bring it to you..."

"Never mind... I'll just deal with it... at least Bazil can visit me every day... right?" Smalls didn't answer me. He just sighed and shook his head no...

"I can't even get visitation?" Now I was mad – and Smalls was about to get it... "This

22

some straight bullshit!" I yelled. Smalls turned around with a 'who the fuck do you think you talkin' to' look on his face – but I didn't give a fuck… "If I were a registered sex offender or a child molester I could see friends, family, and have supervised visits with children…" Smalls tried to get me to quiet down by pointing to the door but I didn't give a fuck… "but they have a bug up their ass when it comes to me and Bazil so instead of going to the bathroom, taking a shit, and flushing the toilet like everyone else – they're denying me visitation – I still have rights dammit!" I screamed. Smalls looked at me with his eyes turned to slits. He stood up, closed his briefcase, and proceeded to walk past me… "Where the fuck do you think you're going?" I asked…

"I don't have to put up with this shit!" he yelled.

"Are you fuckin' kidding me right now? I'm stuck in here – my bail was revoked – I can't get any visitation – and you're mad because I'm upset?"

"I told you about comin' at me like that…"

"You're the only person I'm allowed to talk to!"

"I didn't do this shit to you!"

"I never said you did – but you're my attorney – and my rights are being violated – and I can't defend myself…" I said with tears in my eyes…

"You're right… I'm sorry…" Smalls said as he sat back down… "I'm just not in a good place right now…"

"What's wrong?"

"It has nothing to do with you…"

"I know…"

"Let's get back to your situation…"

"Let's not…"

"Beautiee… I can't sit here all day…"

"The hell you can't," I laughed "You're the only one I have permission to talk to… and I have questions… and you get paid by the hour… so let's talk…"

"Well… you can't see Bazil because…"

"Smalls?" I interrupted…

"Yes Beautiee?"

"What's wrong?" I asked as I took his hand. Smalls didn't answer me right away. His eyes started tearing up and I wrapped my arm around him…

"She wants a divorce…" I didn't say anything. I just kept my arm around him and held his hand… "I wish she was more like you…" he whispered…

"Me?" I asked in surprise…

"You love Bazil with everything in you – you're willing to fight for him… and you'll drag a Bitch with the quickness if a Bitch try and take him…" he laughed…

"Damn right I will…" I laughed…

"Don't tell Bazil…"

"Why not?"

"I don't want him to know…"

"That's your brother…"

"I know…"

"He'll be there for you…"

"I know… that's what I'm afraid of…"

"Why would you be afraid to let Bazil be there for you?"

"Because… he told her if she ever hurt me… he'd kill her…" I didn't respond. I just continued to hold his hand for a few moments… and then I changed the subject…

"So why can't I see Bazil?"

"When you're incarcerated, visitor's need to fill out an application. Once the application is approved, they're put on the list of approved visitors."

"That's bullshit – I didn't need to fill out an application to go see my cousin when he got locked up!"

"You're in here for 3 capital offenses Beautiee."

"I know…"

"So Bazil's application was denied for two reasons…"

"Okay…"

"He had a prior conviction… and… because he served time in this facility…" Smalls hesitated…

"What is it Smalls?"

"He's considered a security risk…" Smalls sighed.

"Can they do this?"

"Yes Beautiee… they can…"

"When's my next court date?"

"They're in the process of selecting jurors now…"

"How long will it take?"

"Connecticut isn't like other states…"

"I don't understand…"

"Connecticut has something called 'Individual Voir Dire' – this means the lawyers on both sides are allowed to question jurors individually and outside the presence of other jurors. It helps us exclude people we think are bias or can't be impartial."

"That can be to my benefit right?"

"If you were married to anybody but Bazil…" Smalls sighed.

"Oh my God…" I whispered.

"Have a little faith Beautiee…" Smalls said as he took my hand…

"How much longer?" I asked with tears in my eyes…

"We should be done in about a week…"

"So then I'll go to trial soon?"

"It could be a couple of weeks… or a couple of months…"

"Oh my God…"

"I'll do everything I can Beautiee…"

"How's Bazil?"

"Honestly… I'd rather be here with you…"

"That bad huh?"

"That bad…"

"You almost done in there?" The officer yelled…

"Why?" Smalls asked…

"You been in there a long time…"

"So what?"

"So she isn't entitled to preferential treatment – she needs to be back in her cell…"

"You got somewhere you need to be?"

"As a matter-of-fact… I do…"

"Sucks to be you then – I'll be done when I'm done!" Smalls yelled. I put my hand over my mouth to keep from laughing out loud. "Do you have any more questions?" Smalls asked…

"No…"

"Is there anything else I can do for you?"

"Yes…" I answered as I stood up and pulled him into a hug…

"I love you too Beautiee…"

"Smalls?"

"Yes Beautiee?"

"If she can't see what a good man you are… she doesn't deserve you…" I said as I kissed him on the cheek…

"Thank you Beautiee – Yo guard – I'm done…"

"'Bout fuckin' time!" he growled as he opened the door…

"Beautiee – I'll see you soon – have a good evening officer – what's your name?"

"Thompson…"

"What's your first name?"

"Good night Mr. Smalls," he answered ignoring Smalls question as he closed the door behind him and came towards me…

"Ummmmm… shouldn't I be going back to my cell?" I asked nervously…

"What's your hurry?" he asked as he walked me backwards into the corner…"

"Well… I thought you had somewhere to be… I wouldn't want to hold you up…"

"Mmmmm… you're beautiful… most women come in here and look like shit without make-up… but you… you're a natural beauty…" he said as he came closer. I couldn't move. He leaned in to kiss me and I tried to be gentle as I pushed him away from me…

"Thank you… I appreciate the compliment… maybe I should go back to my cell now…"

"In a bit… I'd like to get better acquainted…" he whispered as he pulled me into a kiss…

"I'm not interested in getting better acquainted!" I snapped as I pushed him away from me…

"Let me make myself clear…" he said as he pushed me back into the corner… "I didn't ask you if you were interested in getting better acquainted – I said I'd like to get better acquainted!" He pulled me into a kiss again, sliding his hands up and down my back and down to my ass...

"My husband is going to have a problem with us getting acquainted..." I said as I pushed him away from me again...

"Fuck your husband – as long as you're in here – I'm your husband! Do I make myself clear?" he asked as he came towards me again...

"Perfectly..." I whispered...

"Good... now bring your ass here..." he said as he pulled me into a hug and started kissing me on my neck... "So... just to be clear... who's your husband?" he asked as he began massaging my breast...

"Bazil Osgood..." I answered with tears in my eyes...

"Oh my God... I'm... I'm sorry... he gasped as he backed away from me... "Let's get you back to your cell – come with me..." he stammered as he flew out the room. I ran down the corridor to catch up to him... "What's your hurry?" I thought you wanted to get better acquainted?"

"I got somewhere I gotta be!" he stammered as he hurried to unlock the cell..."

"Good night Officer Thompson..."

"Good night Mrs. Osgood!" he said as he locked the cell and hurried down the corridor.

Chapter 4

"What's up now Bitch!" Burly yelled as she slammed the chair down on my head. Unbeknownst to Burly and everyone else, I'd had much practice in falling down while drunk only to get back up and laugh it off... and this dizziness I was feeling as I hit the floor was nothing compared to the rage that was boiling in my blood ever since she tried me...

"You tell me!" I screamed maniacally as I slid underneath the table, brought it up with my body, slammed it down on her, and stood on top of it, using the legs of the table as leverage so she couldn't get out from under it...

"Help... I can't breathe..." she choked as Deputy Warden Hein came running into the rec room...

"Get your ass down from there!" he yelled as he yanked me down off the table and threw me to the floor. I was enraged but I wasn't crazy enough to fight the Deputy Warden so I stayed right where he threw me and watched him lift the table up off Burly and console her...

"I'on know why she fuckin' wit' me!" she cried...

"Please – spare me the crocodile tears – you've been in the middle of shit since you got here..." he sighed as he shooed her away from him...

"That's fucked up! You must be fuckin' her!" she screamed...

"Thompson – take her to solitary!" Deputy Warden Hein yelled as he came towards me...

"You alright?" he asked as he extended his hand to help me up off the floor...

"I'll live..." I answered...

"You're bleeding – I'm taking you to the infirmary..." he said as he took me by the arm and escorted me out the rec room and down the corridor... "Listen to me..." he said as he turned me to face him and pushed me against the wall by my shoulders... "I'm trying to look out for you as best I can – but you can't afford to catch another charge – understand?"

"Yea..."

"I'll keep Burly in solitary for now but the max is 15 days – if you're still in here you have to avoid her at all costs..."

"How am I supposed to do that?"

"When you're in the rec room – make sure you're always facing the entrance – this way if she comes for you – you'll see her coming – she can't sneak you as long as you're facing her..."

"Okay..."

"I'm taking you to the infirmary – after you get checked out – you'll go back to your cell – unless you need to be taken to the hospital…"

"I hope not – my husband won't be happy about this…"

"Oh I already know…" he said as he escorted me into the infirmary…

"Nurse?"

"Yes Deupty?"

"Make sure she's okay – she needs to be in court tomorrow," he answered on his way out the door…

"Waaaiiitttt!" I yelled…

"Yes Beautiee?"

"I'm going to court tomorrow?"

"As long as you don't need to go the hospital – matter-of-fact – nurse, she's got an injury to her head – keep her here for tonight…"

"Yes sir…" the nurse acknowledged as she patted the bed for me to sit on so she could check my vitals…

"I'm going to court tomorrow…" I beamed as she took my blood pressure…

"Don't get your hopes up sweetie – you'll be back here tomorrow night…"

"Fuck you…" I thought to myself as she checked to see if I needed stiches. I couldn't contain my excitement.

"Make yourself comfortable – try to get some sleep…" she said as she propped a few pillows behind my head after pushing me back to lay down. I closed my eyes as if I were going to sleep and began fantasizing about Bazil...

Chapter 5

"Let's go Beautiee!" the nurse yelled as she turned on that bright neon light. I almost forgot where I was until I opened my eyes... "Deputy Hein will be here to escort you to breakfast – I'll see you later," she said as she went over to another prisoner...

"Well good morning to you too... Bitch..." I thought to myself as I jumped down off the bed and went towards the door...

"Good morning Beautie – I hope you got some sleep – let's get you some breakfast..." Deputy Warden Hein said as he took me by the arm and escorted me down the corridor and past the rec room. I wasn't sure what was going on but I didn't ask questions – I just allowed him to lead me into another room with other prisoners... "Wait here – I'll be right back..." he said as he left the room...

"Hey... What's going on?" I asked a woman sitting next to me.

"We're all going to court," she answered.

"Oh... okay...," I smiled.

"I hope you like fried bacon, egg, and cheese on a roll 'cause that's all they had on the truck – and coffee light and sweet – this ain't a fuckin' restaurant so make due..." Deputy Warden Hein said as he placed a box of sandwiches and a box of coffees on the table...

"Oh my God – that smells so good!" I exclaimed as I took a sandwich and a cup of coffee...

"This is your first time huh?" she asked...

"Yea..." I answered as I started chewing...

"Hot damn! These virgins get younger and prettier," she laughed...

"Oh please – I'm nobody's virgin..." I laughed.

"I'm not talkin' about your virginity!" she laughed, "I'm talkin' about this being the first time you've been in jail! Haaaa..... Haaaaa....."

"Leave her alone Mary!" another woman said...

"It's okay..." I said... "I can't believe I thought you were talkin' about my virginity..." I laughed.

"What's your name pretty?" she asked.

"Beautiee."

"No shit! Your mother actually named you that?"

"Yea..."

"Well I'm Mary – it's nice to meet you..." she said as she extended her hand...

"Nice meeting you too..." I said as I shook her hand and started drinking coffee...

"Beautiee – let's go – now!" Deputy Warden Hein ordered as he walked back into the room. I stood up immediately, waiting for him to escort me to wherever I was going next. He took me by my arm and escorted me to another room, pushed me inside, came into the room, and closed the door behind him... "Sit down!" he ordered as he pointed to one of the chairs. He sat down in the other chair before he continued... "Stay away from Mary...

"Did I do something wrong?"

"Listen to me Beautiee – Mary's been in here for a long time – she gets cozy with newbies, gets them to trust her, then reports what she learns to the D.A. for perks and favors..."

"Okay..."

"Finish your coffee – you'll all be cuffed together when you leave here – you'll step up into the van – and you'll all sit together until we got to the court house – once we get to the court house you'll be escorted off the van and into the waiting room – once you get in the waiting room you'll be un-cuffed; however, when you're called you'll be re-cuffed with your hands in front of you and I'll escort you to the Bailiff. The Bailiff will sit you down at the table with your attorney and then your cuffs will come off.

"Will my husband be there?'

"I'm sure he'll be in the court room but he can't sit with you and your attorney."

"Okay..." I sighed...

"Listen to me Beautiee – and this is very important – I need you to behave yourself – no outbursts – no flailing arms and hands – and whatever you do – don't open your mouth unless instructed – you hear me?"

"Yea..."

"Okay – now let's go..." he said as he stood up, grabbed my arm, and escorted me back into the room with Mary and the others so we could get cuffed. When we got to the courthouse it was extremely chaotic – "This way! Hurry Up! Move!" They didn't give a damn that we were cuffed together – they just wanted us outta the way...

"Beautiee..." I heard... so I turned to look...

"Hey Keisha!" I beamed...

"We'll be inside..." she mouthed as she pointed to Courtroom A...

"Move it!" Deputy Warden Hein yelled as he pushed me into everyone else in front of me. When we got inside the waiting room he removed the cuffs before he spoke... "Sorry I was kinda rough – please don't take it personal – they're watching us all like a hawk – they have cameras and eyes everywhere – and Beautiee – don't ever speak to anyone you see coming or going – that's

the worst thing you could possibly do to yourself –
understand?"

"Yea…"

"Okay – Beautiee – you're up – stand up
and extend your arms out in front of you…" He
waited for me to do as instructed and then he
cuffed my wrists before he continued… "I'm going
to take you into the court room – the Bailiff will
escort you to the table with your attorney – do
you remember what we talked about?"

"Yea…"

"Okay then – let's go…" he said as he
grabbed me by the arm and escorted me to the
court room. Once inside, the Bailiff grabbed me
by the arm and started to escort me to the table
where Smalls was waiting for me with a smile, as
well as the judge and the jury. I had all
intentions of behaving myself but as soon as I
saw Bazil my intentions went out the window
along with my common sense…

"Bailiff! Get him!" the judge yelled as
Bazil ran towards me and grabbed me up in his
arms. Instinctively I lifted my arms over Bazil's
head and wrapped my legs around his waist
which cause us to fall to the floor… "Bailiff!
What the hell's a matter with you! I said get
him!" Bazil and I were kissing profusely. He was
the oxygen I needed and in that moment I didn't
give a damn about the judge, the Bailiff, or the
jury – I was breathing – for the first time in days
I could breathe without being afraid it would be

my last breath – for the first time in days I could breathe in... breathe out... and breath in again. Bazil held me against him as we continued kissing and my cuffed wrists were underneath him so there was no way the Bailiff could follow the judge's order. Two officers came running down towards the bench as the Bailiff turned us on our side so he could un-cuff me and pull us apart...

"Please... don't hurt her!" Bazil cried as the court officers grabbed Bazil...

"You're the one that hurt your wife by pulling a stunt like that in my court room! Get 'em both outta here!" Judge Duffey boomed. Smalls stood up to plead my case but Bazil began pleading before he could...

"Your honor... please... I'm begging you..."

"You can fill out an application for visitation like everybody else..."

"My application was denied..." Bazil said as he started to cry. The court officers loosened their grip but didn't let him go...

"Is this true?" Judge Duffey asked Prosecutor Beverly...

"Yes it is..." Smalls answered...

"I'm not asking you Smalls..."

"Yes Your Honor..." Smalls acknowledged as he sat down...

"Yes – it's true Your Honor..." Beverly acknowledged. Judge Duffey sighed and shook his head before continuing...

"Mr. Osgood – when was the last time you saw your wife?"

"I haven't seen her since she was arrested..." Bazil answered while tears streamed down his face. No one said anything for a few moments. Judge Duffey shook his head, put his head in his hands, and then stood up before he spoke...

"Courts in recess – Smalls – Cogswell – in my chambers – Bailiff hold the defendant – Mr. Osgood – go to the back and sit down – jurors please return to the waiting area until you're asked to return...

I watched as Judge Duffey came back into the court room along with the attorneys. Smalls walked past me and winked as he went to the table and sat down. After the prosecutor sat down the Bailiff spoke:

"All rise." Everyone stood up. "Department One of the Superior Court is now in session. Judge Duffey presiding. Please be seated."

Judge Duffey spoke... "Bailiff – please escort the jurors back into the court room. The Bailiff did as he was instructed. "Mr. Osgood – approach the bench." Bazil walked up to the bench and stood without speaking... "Mr. Osgood – you can remain in the court room as long as I don't hear a peep out of you – you are not to speak unless you are called to testify – other than that I don't want to hear a word from you – and I especially don't want another spectacle like I saw earlier – am I clear?"

"Yes Your Honor..." Bazil answered.

"Glad to hear it – now go sit in the back. The judge waited for Bazil to go sit down and then he spoke again... "Good morning, ladies and gentlemen. Calling the case of the People of the State of Connecticut versus Beautiee Osgood. Are both sides ready?"

"Ready for the People, Your Honor..." Beverly said.

"Ready for the Defense, Your Honor..." Smalls said.

"Will the clerk please swear in the jury?" Judge Duffey asked...

"Will the jury please stand and raise your right hand?" The clerk asked. After the jurors were standing she continued... "Do each of you swear that you will fairly try the case before this court, and that you will return a true verdict according to the evidence and the instructions of the court, so help you, God? Please say "I do". The jurors said "I do" unison. "You may be seated."

Chapter 6

Beverly's Opening Statement

"Your Honor and ladies and gentlemen of the jury,

The defendant has been charged with the attempted murder of her husband, Bazil Osgood, the murder of Sonia Santos, and the murder of Trevor Joseph. The evidence will show that on January 13, 2019, the defendant invited her lover, Sonia Santos over to her home as well as her husband's lover, Trevor Joseph to set them all up to be killed. The evidence will also show that her husband, Bazil Osgood, her lover, Sonia Santos, and her husband's lover, Trevor Joseph, were all shot with the same gun. The defendant's fingerprints were on the gun used to shoot her husband, Bazil Osgood, her lover, Sonia Santos, and her husband's lover, Trevor Joseph. The evidence I present will prove to you that the defendant is guilty as charged."

Smalls's Opening Statement

"Your Honor and ladies and gentlemen of the jury,

Under the law my client is presumed innocent until proven guilty. During this trial, you will hear no real evidence against my client. You will come to know the truth: that my client, Beautiee Osgood, loves her husband. You will also find out that my client invited her lover, Sonia Santos, over to have a threesome with her husband – she did not invite her lover over to kill her, nor did she intend to kill her husband. You will also find out that her husband's lover, Trevor Joseph, was never invited. You will also come to know that my client shot her husband's lover, Trevor Joseph, because she feared for her life – especially after he shot her husband – therefore; my client is not guilty."

"Beverly – you may call your first witness..." Judge Duffey said.

"Thank you Your Honor – I call Joselyn Logan."

"Oh shit!" I heard someone say from the back of the court room. I looked straight ahead but I could feel Bazil watching me and I knew he was worried about what Joselyn was going to say...

"Please state your name for the record…" Judge Duffey instructed…

"Joselyn Logan."

"Please raise your right hand and place your left hand on the bible…" Judge Duffey instructed as the court clerk held the Bible… "Do you swear, under penalty of perjury, that the testimony you are about to give shall be the truth, the whole truth, and nothing but the truth?"

"I swear, under penalty of perjury, that the testimony I am about to give shall be the truth, the whole truth, and nothing but the truth."

"Thank you Joselyn – but in the future – you can simply answer I do…"

"Oh – Okay – I thought I was already married!" Joselyn laughed along with the jurors and everyone else in the court room… except Beverly…

"That was funny Joselyn – however – this is not – understand?" Beverly retorted…

"Objection – that's a witness – not her child…" Small said.

"I know that's right!" Keisha yelled out before quickly putting her hand ovr her mouth…

"Sustained – easy Beverly…" Judge Duffey ordered…

"Mrs. Logan where you at work on December 17, 2018?"

"Yes I was."

"Did you witness an altercation between the defendant and MaryJane LaRue?"

"Yes... I did..."

"Please tell the court what you witnessed..."

"Well... I'm sorry Mrs. Osgood..."

"Your Honor – please instruct the witness to address the court and not the defendant..." Beverly said.

"Mrs. Logan – please address the court and not the defendant..." Judge Duffey ordered...

"Okay..." Joselyn answered as tears streamed down her cheeks. Sam ran up to the witness box to give his wife a tissue and console her...

"Are you okay to continue?" Judge Duffey asked as Sam went to sit back down...

"Yes Your Honor..." Joselyn answered...

"Very well – please answer the question..." Judge Duffey ordered. Joselyn sighed before continuing...

"Mrs. Osgood dragged MaryJane down the hall by her hair... and threw her out the door..." Most of the jury gasped – some of them laughed...

"Did the defendant say anything to MaryJane LaRue after she was thrown out?" Beverly asked. Joselyn started crying again before answering...

"Mrs. Osgood told her if she caught her on the premises again... she would kill her..."

The jury gasped again...

"Mrs. Logan – to clarify – is it your testimony that the defendant threatened MaryJane LaRue and told her she would kill her if she were caught back on the premises?"

"Yes…" Joselyn acknowledged.

"Thank you Mrs. Logan – nothing further…" Beverly said as she looked over at Smalls and then said, "Your Witness…" before sitting down.

"How are you Mrs. Logan?" Smalls asked as he stood up…

"I'm okay…"

"Can I get you some water?"

"No thank you…"

"Okay – Mrs. Logan – prior to the altercation you witnessed with the defendant – did you have a conversation with MaryJane LaRue?"

"Yes I did…"

"Where did this conversation take place?"

"In the ladies room."

"Did you discuss the defendant?"

"Yes we did."

"What – if anything – did MaryJane LaRue say to you in the ladies room?"

"She called Mrs. Osgood a Bitch and she said she was going to have to check Mrs. Osgood and put her in her place like she did Mr. Osgood's first wife." The jury gasped… Smalls smiled along with Joselyn's husband Sam and Bazil as

Beverly put her head in her hands before Smalls continued...

"Did anyone hear your conversation in the ladies room?"

"Yes."

"Who heard your conversation?"

"My mother and Mrs. Osgood."

"Mrs. Logan – to be clear – is it your testimony that your mother and the defendant heard your conversation in the ladies room?"

"Yes."

"Hmmmmm... I would'a threw her ass out too..." Smalls mumbled...

"Objection – move to strike!" Beverly yelled...

"Objection sustained – the jury will disregard that last comment – Smalls don't ever do that in my court..."

"Yes Your Honor – I apologize..." Smalls smirked as he looked at Beverly and sat down.

"Re-direct?" Judge Duffey asked.

"No Your Honor..." Beverly answered...

"The witness may be excused..." Judge Duffey said. Joselyn got up from the witness box and joined her husband behind Smalls.

"I'm proud of you..." Sam whispered as he took her hand...

"Really? I didn't want to say all that..." Joselyn whispered. Bazil put his hand on Joselyn's shoulder and smiled...

"Mr. Osgood – please move to the back of the court as you were instructed earlier – don't let me have to remind you again!" Judge Duffey growled...

"Yes Your Honor – sorry..." Bazil said as he got up and went to the back of the court room with Troy & Keisha. Judge Duffy watched as Keisha took Bazil's hand for a few moments before he spoke...

"Court will be in recess for 30 minutes – Bailiff – please escort the jurors to the waiting room – everyone else may remain seated in the court room or you can go out for coffee..." Judge Duffey said as he got up and left the bench to go to his chambers...

"You okay?" Smalls whispered to me so Beverly couldn't hear our conversation...

"I'm fine..." I sighed.

"I know you're happy 'cause you got to see Bazil but you need to stay focused – don't smile – don't do anything – just sit here... with me..." he whispered as he pulled me into a hug and slipped me a pad and pen as if he was reading my mind...

"Hey My Thirst Quencher..." I wrote...

"I'm sorry to tell you this – but after my arrest, Smalls came to see me. When he left – Officer Thompson came in the room to see me. I asked to go back to my cell but Officer Thompson said he wanted to get better acquainted. I told him my husband wouldn't like it but he said fuck your husband – while you're in here – I'm your husband! I pushed him away from me but he grabbed me, he kissed me, and told me he wasn't asking my permission... and then he groped my breast! As he was feeling my breast he asked me if he made himself clear and I told him he made himself perfectly clear. He asked me again who my husband was but instead of saying his name I said your name – he got scared, apologized, and hurried me back to my cell. I didn't report it and I don't want to report it – I'm already going through enough dealing with the Burly Bitch who tried to push up on me talkin' 'bout she was going to fuck me with a dildo but instead she chose to hit me upside my head with a chair because I embarrassed her ass – don't worry too much about that – I brought a table down on top of her and Deputy Warden Hein put her in solitary so she won't fuck with me again for the moment – I love you so much – I'm trying to be strong but I don't know how much more I can take." When I finished writing, I slid the pad and pen back to Smalls...

"You need to report this mutha fucka!" Smalls wrote before passing the pad back to me... I snatched the pen and responded... "No!" and then slammed the pen down on the pad...

"Miss – please return to your seat until you're called as a witness..." the Bailiff ordered...

"Shit!" Keisha said as she went to sit back down. Bazil watched intently as Smalls tore the paper off the pad, folded it, and put it in his left pocket. Smalls then took a pencil out of his briefcase, went across the paper with the pencil to highlight all the imprints on the page, tore that paper off the pad, and put it in his right pocket...

"I'll be right back – I'm going to the bathroom..." Smalls said deliberately...

"I need to go too – I haven't used the bathroom since I drank coffee..." I said just as deliberately...

"You can't go right now..." the Bailiff said...

"Please – I won't run – I just need to pee – you have cameras everywhere..."

"Very well – I'll escort you to the bathroom..." he said as he walked over to the table and un-cuffed me...

"Really?" Smalls said, agitated... "I'll escort my client to the bathroom!"

"Sir – I can't let you do that..." the Bailiff said...

"He's right..." Beverly added...

"Yo – check it – I'm taking my client to the fuckin' bathroom – to pee! Let's go Beautiee!" Smalls said as he snatched me by the arm, pulled me up out the chair, and marched me down towards the back of the court room, past Bazil,

Keisha, Troy, Sam, and Joselyn – and out the door into the corridor...

"Hey – wait a minute – you can't do that!" another Bailiff yelled...

"What? What the fuck am I doing? I'm her attorney! Do you really think I would jeopardize my client's freedom?" Smalls yelled...

"I'm sorry sir – she needs to be escorted inside the bathroom and out..." the Bailiff said...

"And I'll do that – now can we go or should she just pee right here?"

"Fine – but make sure she doesn't try anything..."

"Whatever – c'mon Beautiee – hurry up 'cause I gotta pee too..." Smalls said as he deliberately pushed me into the men's room... "Listen – go down to the last stall and close the door – hopefully Bazil will get the hint and come look for you – give him this..." he said as he handed me the paper form his right pocket... "I'm going to wait by the door to make sure you don't try anything – but I gotta pee first – and if you really gotta pee – leave it in the toilet in case they wanna check..." he laughed as he went into another stall...

"Shit – Smalls you in here?" Bazil asked as he came into the men's room...

"Yea Bazil – I'll be out in a minute..." Smalls answered... and then Bazil saw me as I came out the stall...

"Beautiee…" Bazil said as he came towards me…"

"Hey my Thirst Quencher…" I sighed as we fully embraced. Bazil began kissing me forcefully and I had no objection. I opened my mouth further and welcomed his tongue. Bazil moved his right arm up, pulled me closer with his left, and bent me back on the sink as we continued kissing feverishly…

"Beautiee – let's go – they'll come looking for us…" Smalls said as he started tugging at my arm…

"I love you so much it hurts…" Bazil said as he continued to hold me…

"I love you too…" I said as I put the folded paper Smalls gave me into Bazil's pocket…

"Beautiee – we gotta go…" Smalls said, tugging at my arm…

"We're gonna get through this Beautiee…" Bazil said as he kissed me again…"

"You promise?" I asked as I kissed him back…

"I promise…" Bazil answered as he kissed me again…

"And you never make a promise you can't keep… right?" I asked through tear-soaked eyes…

"Right…" Bazil answered as he kissed my eyes and my tears…

"Beautiee…" Smalls said as he tugged my arm again…

"I'm coming..." I sighed as I let go of Bazil and allowed Smalls to escort me back to the court room...

"All rise..."the Bailiff said. Everyone stood up. "Department One of the Superior Court is now in session. Judge Duffey presiding. Please be seated."

"Calling the case of the People of the State of Connecticut versus Beautiee Osgood. Are both sides ready?"

"Ready for the People, Your Honor..." Beverly said.

"Ready for the Defense, Your Honor..." Smalls said.

"Welcome back Mrs. Osgood," Judge Duffey said sarcastically...

"I'm sorry Your Honor – I had to pee..." The jurors laughed along with Keisha, Troy, Sam, and Joselyn...

"Since your husband's not here, I'm guessing that's not all you had to do..." Judge Duffey said. I didn't say anything – I just sat down smiling... "I don't like to be kept waiting..." Judge Duffey said...

"It won't happen again Your Honor..." Smalls said...

"It better not..."

"Yes Your Honor."

"Beverly – are you ready to call your next witness?"

"Yes Your Honor – I call Sheila Henley." We all watched as Sheila went to the witness box.

"Please state your name for the record..." Judge Duffey instructed...

"Sheila Henley."

"Please raise your right hand and place your left hand on the bible..." Judge Duffey instructed as the court clerk held the bible... "Do you swear, under penalty of perjury, that the testimony you are about to give shall be the truth, the whole truth, and nothing but the truth?"

"I will..." Sheila said as she sat down.

"I guess you're already married?" Judge Duffey asked...

"I am..."

"Very well – Beverly – you may proceed..."

"Mrs. Henley – earlier today, Mrs. Logan testified that you over-heard a conversation between her and MaryJane LaRue – is that true?" Beverly asked...

"Yes it is..." Sheila answered...

"Would you please tell the court and the jury what you specifically heard?"

"I specifically heard MaryJane LaRue call Mrs. Osgood a Bitch and I specifically heard MaryJane LaRue tell my daughter that she was going to have to check Mrs. Osgood and put her in her place like she did Mr. Osgood's first wife."

"You didn't like MaryJane LaRue did you?"

"Objection..." Smalls said.

"Overruled – the witness may answer..." Judge Duffey ordered...

"No I didn't..."

"Could you please explain to the court why you didn't like MaryJane LaRue?"

"She was lazy, she passed most of her work to my daughter, and she walked around like she owned the place..."

"I see – what was Ms. LaRue's title?"

"The same as my daughter – Personal Assistant."

"Was Mr. Osgood having an affair with Ms. LaRue?"

"Objection!" Smalls yelled...

"Sustained..." Judge Duffey acknowledged...

"Withdrawn..." Beverly said... and then she continued... "Your daughter was promoted after Ms. LaRue was thrown out – wasn't she?"

"Yes she was..."

"Hmmmmm... how convenient..." Beverly said sarcastically...

"It had nothing to do with convenience – my daughter is loyal, dedicated, and works hard – she earned that promotion!"

"Isn't it true that your son-in-law – Samuel Logan – is also the Vice President of Osgood Publishing?"

"Yes – that's true..."

"So – to make sure I understand you correctly – your son-in-law is the Vice President at Osgood Publishing – your daughter – who also works there – gets promoted right after Ms. LaRue gets thrown out – and you never liked her – and you don't think any of this is a coincidence?"

"No – I don't think any of that is a coincidence…"

"Hmmmmm… interesting – your witness…" Beverly said to Smalls as she sat down…

"Mrs. Henley – you testified that you over-heard the conversation in the bathroom between Ms. LaRue and your daughter – is that correct?"

"Yes it is…"

"Did you have any prior knowledge that Ms. LaRue felt animosity towards Mrs. Osgood?"

"Objection!" Beverly yelled.

"Overruled – the witness may answer…" Judge Duffey ordered…

"No I did not…"

"Did you know Ms. LaRue was in the bathroom?"

"No I did not…"

"Did Mrs. Osgood tell you that she was planning on promoting your daughter?"

"No she did not."

"Prior to Mrs. Osgood throwing Ms. LaRue out – did you have any discussion regarding Ms. LaRue with Mrs. Osgood, Mr. Osgood, or your son-in-law?"

"No I did not…"

"Thank you Mrs. Henley – I have no further questions..." Smalls said as he sat down...

"The witness is excused – I'm taking an early lunch – court is closed for lunch – please be back by 1 pm sharp!" Judge Duffey said as he put on his robe, stood up, and went into his chambers. I watched as the jurors exited the court room, then the clerk.

"Everyone needs to leave – court is closed..." the Bailiff ordered. Keisha, Troy, Joselyn, and Sam exited the court room. Bazil was nowhere in sight.

"I wish I could go to lunch too..." I sighed...

"Mrs. Osgood – you need to come with me..." the Bailiff said as he approached me...

"I need to speak with my attorney... please..."

"I'll escort you to the attorney-client room – your attorney can meet you there..." he said as he took me by the arm and pulled me up... "Sorry – I need to cuff you..." he said as he cuffed my hands.

"I'll see you in a few minutes – I'll treat you to lunch – be right back!" Smalls said as he ran out...

"This way Mrs. Osgood..." the Bailiff said as he led me down the corridor past the men's room, to the attorney-client room. "Wait here for your attorney – I'll see you back in the court room..." he said as he left...

"Beautiee…" Bazil whispered as he cracked the door…

"Bazil – don't come in…" I whispered…

"I'm not – I'm waiting for Smalls…"

"Okay…"

"I love you…"

"I love you too…"

"Bazil – you can't be here…" Smalls said…

"I know – I'm leaving – come by the house after court – we'll talk then…" Bazil said…

"Aaight bet – I'll see you tonight…" Smalls said as Bazil went down the hall and left the courthouse… "Okay Beautiee – I got some good ole fashioned comfort food – macaroni & cheese, fried chicken, collard greens, cornbread, and sweet tea…" he said as I tore the lid off and dove in… "I got me a plate too…" Smalls said as he started eating…

"Bazil didn't read my letter yet…"

"I know he didn't – he's too happy…"

"I'm scared…"

"I know – but I think we can beat this…"

"I'm not afraid of that… I'm afraid of Bazil…"

"I'm afraid too – I didn't even want to tell him but I had too – I'd wanna know if it was my wife…"

"He'd never forgive you if you didn't tell him…"

"That too…" he laughed… "But Beautiee – you need to file a complaint…"

"I can't…"

"Yes you can – I'll be with you every step of the way…"

"You can't be with me 24 hours…"

"I'll get you protective custody…"

"I'm already in hell – imagine what they'll do to me if I report it? I just wanna get through this so I can go home…" I said as I started to cry…

"I know Beautiee – I gotchu…" he said as he handed me a napkin – but once Bazil reads your letter they'll know…"

"So what?"

"So you can't afford to have your husband back in prison…"

"I know that too – what am I supposed to do?"

"Le'me ask you something – why didn't you tell me what was going on with Burly?" I bust out laughing… "What's so funny?"

"The way you say Burly…" I laughed…

"Is that her name?"

"That's my name for her – and when you see her – that'll be your name for her too – she makes Buckwheat from the Alphalfas look sexy!" I laughed…

"Damn – that's fucked up!" Smalls laughed – but I'm glad you fucked her up…"

"I had no choice – she would've kept coming for me…"

"Well – since Deputy Hein is lookin' out I won't push that issue – but Officer Thompson needs his ass beat!"

"Oh it's comin'!" I laughed...

"I know – that's what I'm afraid of...It's 12:45 – let's get back before everyone else..." Smalls said as he got up to leave the room...

"Good idea – thanks for lunch..." I said as I got up and we left the room...

"All rise..."the Bailiff said. Everyone stood up. "Department One of the Superior Court is now in session. Judge Duffey presiding. Please be seated."

"Calling the case of the People of the State of Connecticut versus Beautiee Osgood. Are both sides ready?"

"Ready for the People, Your Honor..." Beverly said.

"Ready for the Defense, Your Honor..." Smalls said.

"Thank you all for being prompt..." Judge Duffey said as he sat down... Beverly – you may call your next witness..."

"Thank you Your Honor – I call Detective Katina Jones."

Chapter 7

"Please state your name for the record..." Judge Duffey instructed...

"Katina Jones."

"Please raise your right hand and place your left hand on the bible..." Judge Duffey instructed as the court clerk held the Bible... "Do you swear, under penalty of perjury, that the testimony you are about to give shall be the truth, the whole truth, and nothing but the truth?"

"I do..." Detective Jones said as she sat down.

"Very well – Beverly – you may proceed..."

"Detective Jones – did you receive a call for possible domestic violence at the defendant's address on December 23, 2018 at around 9 p.m.?"

"Yes I did."

"When you arrived, what – if anything did you witness?"

"I received a call for possible domestic violence at the defendant's home. When I arrived, I knocked on the door, asked if I could come in, and I was allowed inside."

"What – if anything – did you observe?"

"The defendant appeared to be upset."

"Did you determine that any domestic violence had occurred?"

"Yes – I did."

"How did you determine that domestic violence had occurred?"

"I asked the defendant if everything was okay and she told me that she and her husband had a fight…" I listened intently as the jurors started whispering…

"Your initial report also indicated that someone heard gun shots – is that true?"

"Yes it is."

"Did you ask the defendant about gun shots specifically?"

"Yes I did."

"What was her response?"

"She told me they were watching Law & Order…" The jurors laughed – but Judge Duffey wasn't amused…

"Did the defendant appear to be hurt?"

"No – she didn't."

"What did you do after you were done with your conversation?"

"I gave her my card, and then I left."

"Thank you Detective – your witness…" Beverly said before she sat down…

"Detective Jones – how are you?" Smalls asked…

"I'm fine…"

"Glad to hear it – on the night in question – did you recover a gun from the defendant's home?"

"No I didn't…" she sighed…

"Was Mr. Osgood home at the time?"

"Yes he was."

"Did he tell you his wife tried to kill him?"

"No he did not."

"Did he want to press charges?"

"No he did not."

"One more question – isn't it true that you told the defendant to be careful because her husband is dangerous?" I smiled as Beverly put her head in her hands and I heard the jurors gasp…

"Yes… that's true – I did tell the defendant that…"

"So – to be clear – it's your testimony that the defendant didn't appear to be hurt – her husband didn't want to press charges – but yet – you warned the defendant to be careful because her husband is dangerous?"

"Yes."

"So – he's dangerous but she's on trial for murder…"

"Objection!" Beverly yelled.

"Sustained…" Judge Duffey said.

"Withdrawn – I'm done!" Smalls said sarcastically as he threw up his hands and sat down…

"The witness is excused – Beverly – you may call your next witness…" Judge Duffey said.

"Thank you Your Honor – I call Beautiee Osgood…" The jury gasped.

"Are you sure you want to do this?" Smalls asked me before I went up to the witness box…

"Yes…" I answered. I was scared but the jury only saw sadness. I could hear the jurors whispering as I went up to the witness box…

"Please state your name for the record…" Judge Duffey instructed…

"Mrs. Beautiee Osgood."

"Please raise your right hand and place your left hand on the bible…" Judge Duffey instructed as the court clerk held the Bible… "Do you swear, under penalty of perjury, that the testimony you are about to give shall be the truth, the whole truth, and nothing but the truth?"

"Yes… I swear…" I said as I sat down.

"Very well – Beverly – you may proceed…"

"How are you Beautiee?" Beverly asked…

"Please call me Mrs. Osgood…"

"Very well – on the first night Detective Jones came to your home – what event transpired?"

"My husband and I were fighting and my neighbor called the police…"

"How you know it was me?" Keisha yelled out. Smalls laughed along with the jury.

"What were you fighting about?"

"Bazil..." I whispered as I began to tear up...

"Mr. Osgood – please go back to your seat!" Judge Duffey ordered.

"I'm just giving my wife some tissues your honor..." Bazil said as he placed the tissues on the table in front of Smalls before returning to the back of the court room with Troy and Keisha.

"We're heading back to the office – call us if you need us..." Sam whispered to Bazil as he got up to leave along with Joselyn and Sheila...

"Your honor – please order the witness to answer the question!" Beverly snapped...

"Please answer the question..." Judge Duffey ordered...

"He... he... cheated on me..." I cried. The jurors gasped. Smalls got up to bring me tissues, and then he sat back at the table...

"Your husband?" Beverly asked...

"Yes..." I answered as I wiped my eyes. I looked toward the back of the court room at Bazil. He was crying and I felt terrible...

"How did you know your husband was cheating on you?"

"I caught them..." I cried.

"Who did you catch your husband cheating on you with?"

"Bazil... I'm sorry..." I cried...

"Your honor..." Beverly started to say...

"Mrs. Osgood – please do not address your husband while giving testimony..." Judge Duffey ordered...

"My husband was cheating on me with Trevor..." I cried. The jurors gasped. I looked towards the back at Bazil. I hated myself but this was necessary – at least I thought so – I prayed so...

"So is it your testimony that you had a fight with your husband because you caught him cheating on you with Trevor?"

"No..."

"Mrs. Osgood – I don't understand..."

"We were fighting because... Bazil was angry with me..."

"Why was your husband angry with you?"

"Because... after I caught Bazil sleeping with Trevor..." I had to stop and gather myself. I kept looking back at Bazil praying he'd forgive me...

"Go on Mrs. Osgood..."

"I slept with Trevor too..." The jurors gasped. I kept looking back at Bazil. He was still crying. I wanted to run to him and beg for forgiveness...

"Wow – I didn't expect that..." Beverly said...

"Is that a question?" Smalls asked.

"Withdrawn – Mrs. Osgood – are you telling us you had a physical altercation with your husband because you slept with his lover?"

"That's part of it..." I answered...

"Please tell the court the other part..." Beverly laughed...

"Objection!" Smalls yelled...

"What's your objection Smalls?" Judge Duffey asked...

"This isn't funny – why is she laughing?"

"Sustained – Mrs. Osgood – please continue..."

"I wanted some wine and I went into the kitchen – but Bazil poured my wine out so I wanted to leave... and Bazil wouldn't let me..."

"What happened next?" Beverly asked...

"Bazil grabbed me... he threw me into the counter... and hurt my back..."

"I'm sorry Beautiee..." Bazil said from the back of the court room...

"Mr. Osgood – please be quiet!" Judge Duffey ordered...

"What – if anything – happened next?" Beverly asked...

"I grabbed a knife out of the holder..." I answered as I started crying again..." and I stabbed him!" I said as I broke down crying. Bazil was crying right along with me.

"I have no further question..." Beverly said with a smile as she sat down... "Your witness..." she said as Smalls got up...

"Here Beautiee..." Smalls said as he handed me some tissues. He waited for me to blow my nose, wipe my tears, and compose myself before he continued… "That was pretty intense – wasn't it?"

"Yes…"

"You testified you stabbed your husband – is that right?"

"Yes… it is…" I answered as I started crying again…

"Where did you stab your husband?"

"I stabbed him… in his hand." The jurors began mumbling…

"Beautiee – I want to make sure the court understood you clearly – is it your testimony that you stabbed your husband in his hand?"

"Yes…"

"Hhmmmmm – if you were trying to kill your husband – you probably would've stabbed him somewhere else – somewhere there's a good chance he'd die…" The jurors began laughing, which angered Beverly…

"Objection!" Beverly yelled…

"Sustained…" Judge Duffey said… "The jury will disregard that last statement…" Judge Duffey said before Smalls continued…

"Beautiee – who left the house first after you had your altercation?"

"Bazil did…"

"So – to be clear – your husband left the house alive?"

"Yes…"

"Your honor – please enter this as an exhibit..." Smalls said as he handed it to Judge Duffey...

"So ordered..." Judge Duffey said and then it was entered into evidence...

"Beautiee – do you know what this is?" Smalls asked. I started crying as soon as I saw it...

"Yes..."

"Please tell the court what it is..."

"It's... the letter I wrote to Bazil... before I left him..." I answered as I broke down crying. Troy held Bazil's hand as he cried along with me...

"Pease read it to the jury..."

"Do I have to?"

"Yes Beautiee... please..."

"Hey my Thirst Quencher," I read before getting choked up. I blew my nose, wiped my tears, and started again... "I'm sorry I hurt you. I love you so much and if I had to marry you all over again, I would. When I married you, I promised you I'd love you forever... and I will... but I can't get that image of you and Trevor out of my head." I looked towards the back of the court room and saw Bazil was crying with me, which made me feel worse. I was just about out of tissues so I used what was left to wipe my nose instead of blowing it before I continued... "I thought I'd feel better after having sex with Trevor but to be honest, I feel like shit. I had sex with Trevor to hurt you because when I saw you with him it broke my heart – because I know you love him too – and I don't know if I can share you or your heart with anyone else. When you asked me to marry you, you promised me you'd make me feel good every day for the rest of my life – and you broke that promise." I had to stop again because I was getting choked up. Smalls was tearing up along with some of the jurors, and Beverly could see that Judge Duffey was touched by what I'd read... "I'm back home. Please give me time. I'll call you when I'm ready. Love, Beautiee."

"I'm sorry Beautiee – I know that wasn't easy..." Smalls said...

"Objection!" Beverly said...

"Overruled..." Judge Duffey said...

"Beautiee – I have one last question for you..." Smalls said...

"Okay..."

"You really love your husband – don't you?"

"Yes..." I cried... "I love you Bazil..."

"I love you too..." Bazil cried as Beverly threw up her hands...

"I have no more questions..." Smalls said as he sat down...

"Mrs. Osgood – you're excused – that's it for today – we'll resume tomorrow at 9 a.m. sharp!" Judge Duffey said as he got up, put on his robe, and left the Bench. I watched as everyone left the court room. I turned to look at the back and Bazil was still sitting there...

"Let's go Beautiee..." the Bailiff said as he started walking towards me...

"Bazil..." I called out to stop him from leaving. Bazil turned around to look at me and I couldn't help myself – I ran right into his arms...

"Smalls – get a hold of your client!" The Bailiff yelled.

"She isn't going anywhere! She's right there in front of you!" Smalls yelled as he watched us...

"I'm sorry..." I cried as he held me...

"You have nothing to be sorry for..." Bazil said before he pulled me into a kiss...

"It's so hard..."

"I know..."

"I miss you..."

"I miss you too..."

"I love you Bazil..."

"I love you too... I'll see you tomorrow..." he said before he kissed me hard. "Please don't cry Beautiee..." he said as he kissed my tears...

"I don't wanna go back to jail..."

"I don't want you to go back either..."

"Beautiee – we gotta go..." Smalls said as he took my hand...

"Okay..." I whispered. The Bailiff came towards me and Bazil went out the court room door.

"How was court?" Mary asked when she saw me...

"It was okay..." I sighed...

"No it wasn't – I can tell by lookin' atcha – what happened?" she asked as she put her arm around me...

"Oh God..." I whispered as I started crying...

"The first day is always hard..." Mary said as she put my head on her shoulder and I continued to cry. Deputy Warden Hein walked over to us and I could see he wasn't too happy but in that moment – Mary was helping me hold it together – maybe she had ulterior motives – maybe she didn't – but I needed her...

"It's so hard..." I cried...

"I know..." Mary acknowledged as she touched my hair...

"I'm all alone in here – I can't see my husband - my friends can't come see me – my parents live down south – the only visit I get is from my attorney..." I cried...

"Why can't your husband come see you?"

"Because my husband is Bazil Osgood..."

"What'd you just say?"

"My husband is Bazil Osgood..."

"Hmmmmm... you'll be alright – I gotta go – hang in there..." she said as she got up and left me...

"Hmmmmm... musta been something I said..." I mumbled...

"That's exactly what it was..." Deputy Warden Hein said...

"Oh God – never mind – I don't even wanna know..." I sighed...

"Well just be careful with her – please!"

"Alright, alright... damn!"

"I'm serious Beautiee – it's for your protection!"

"What the fuck – sorry – what the hell – sorry – dammit – what am I supposed to do?"

"Here – take this – go back to your cell – and don't come out unless you wanna eat!" He snapped as he gave me a note pad and a pen.

"Thank you..." I whispered...

"You're welcome – I'll be leaving soon – I need to see you in my office – come with me..." he said as he pulled me up by my arm and took me down the corridor to his office. When we got to his office, he went in first and sat behind the desk... "Come inside and close the door..."

"Okay..." I said nervously as I closed the door...

"Come sit down in the chair by me..."

"Okay." I sat down and wondered what was going on as he picked up the phone and dialed a number...

"Here..." he said as he handed me the phone...

"Hello?"

"Beautiee..."

"Bazil!"

"You okay?"

"Noo…." I answered as I started crying…

"Please don't cry… you'll make me cry…"

"So…" I laughed. Bazil laughed too. "I love you…

"I love you too…"

"I'll see you tomorrow…"

"Yes… tomorrow…" I sighed… and then Bazil hung up." Thank you…" I said as I reached over to give Deputy Warden Hein a hug…

"Uh uh!"

"I'm sorry…"

"No offense – now let's get you back to your cell – and remember – don't come out unless you're hungry – hopefully this will all be over soon…" he said as he stood up. He waited for me to stand up and when I did, he took me by the arm, escorted me down the corridor, and back to my cell. I made myself comfortable, opened the pad, and starting writing to Bazil:

Love Me Baby

Lovin' at first sight, lovin' me alright,
Lovin' even when things ain't goin' right,
Lovin' me all night 'till the mornin' light,

Love Me Baby

Lovin' me in spite of my many faults,
Lovin' through the hurt, breakin' down my walls,

Lovin' on my heart, kissin' all my scars,

Love Me Baby

Lovin' every day when I've lost my way,
Lovin' me is hard, don't know what to say,
Lovin' let's me know that you wanna stay,

Love Me Baby

Lovin' me in spite of it being hot,
Lovin' all the while even when I'm not,
Lovin' in the dark 'till you find the spot,

Love Me Baby

Lovin' how you touch, and I'm feelin' good,
Lovin' by my side like I knew you could,
Lovin' all along 'till I understood,

Love Me Baby

I tore the song off the pad, folded it, put it in my
top pocket, and went to sleep.

Chapter 8

"All rise…"the Bailiff said. Everyone stood up. "Department One of the Superior Court is now in session. Judge Duffey presiding. Please be seated."

"Good morning, ladies and gentlemen" Judge Duffey said. "Calling the case of the People of the State of Connecticut versus Beautiee Osgood. Are both sides ready?"

"Ready for the People, Your Honor…" Beverly said.

"Ready for the Defense, Your Honor…" Smalls said.

"Mr. Osgood – what are you doing up here – did I not make myself clear?" he snapped as Bazil walked up to the front of the court room…

"Yes Your Honor – you made yourself perfectly clear…" Bazil answered as he walked up to the table where Smalls and I were sitting. The Bailiff stood up, waiting on Judge Duffey's instructions, but Bazil paid him no mind – he came over to me, pulled me up into a hug, and kissed me… "Good morning Beautiee…" he said after he kissed me.

"Good morning…" I breathed. Everyone watched and waited. Bazil let me go and I sat back down next to Smalls. Bazil walked to the back of the court room and sat down with Troy and Keisha. Beverly was annoyed but I didn't give a shit – I was too busy smiling. I took the song I wrote out my pocket and passed it to Smalls. Smalls read it, folded it, and put it in his pocket.

"Your Honor – please excuse me – I'll be right back…" Smalls said as he hurried out the court room. Judge Duffey watched as Smalls left the court room and kept looking to see if Bazil would get up to follow him, but Bazil didn't. When he came back into the court room he saw Judge Duffey stop to look at his watch and used the opportunity to drop the folded paper in Bazil's lap as he walked towards the table…

"Is everything alright?" Judge Duffey asked…

"Yes Your Honor – thanks for asking…" Smalls answered as he sat down next to me…

"Do you need a recess?"

"No Your Honor…"

"Does anyone else need to be excused? Does anyone need to use the bathroom? All good? Good – Beverly – please call your next witness…"

"I'm re-calling Detective Katina Jones…" Beverly said as she stood up. Bazil started reading as Katina took the stand…

"Please state your name for the record…" Judge Duffey instructed…

"Katina Jones."

"Please raise your right hand and place your left hand on the bible…" Judge Duffey instructed as the court clerk held the Bible… "Do you swear, under penalty of perjury, that the testimony you are about to give shall be the truth, the whole truth, and nothing but the truth?"

"I do…" Detective Jones said as she sat down.

"Very well – Beverly – you may proceed…"

"Detective Jones – please tell us what happened when you were called to the defendant's home on January 13, 2019…"

"An ambulance was dispatched to the defendant's home. An attempted homicide was called in along with two other homicides. I was the first to arrive on the scene."

"Could you describe it for us?"

"It was horrific. There was blood everywhere. The neighbors were in the bedroom with the defendant. At first, I couldn't tell who was bleeding or who shot who."

"Do you see the neighbors in the court?"
"Yes."

"Could you point them out for the jury?" Detective Jones pointed to the back of the court room at Troy and Keisha. "Your Honor – please note that Detective Jones pointed out Troy and Keisha Cochran."

"So noted – continue…" Judge Duffey acknowledged.

"Please tell us what happened next…" Beverly said…

"When I got there I was questioning the officers outside. As I was questioning them, they were loading Bazil Osgood's body onto the stretcher and into the ambulance. They closed the door to the ambulance and started to drive off. Mrs. Osgood came running out wearing a robe. She was screaming for Mr. Osgood and I could see she was covered in blood. She pushed me down and kept screaming for Mr. Osgood and kept running towards the ambulance. The ambulance stopped, she got in, and they drove off."

"You testified the defendant pushed you – is that correct?"

"Yes."

"Did you feel threatened by the defendant?"

"No."

"Okay what happened next?"

"I went into the house and their neighbor, Troy Cochran, was in the bedroom."

"Were you able to question him?"

"No."

"Why not?"

"He wouldn't answer any questions."

"Did he offer an explanation?"

"No he didn't."

"So you weren't able to question him."

"Not at that moment."

"What happened next?"

"I began questioning the officers and I noticed two more bodies and a gun."

"Please tell the court who the deceased victims are."

"Sonia Santos and Trevor Joseph."

"Is this the gun you recovered from the crime scene?"

"Yes – that's the gun..."Katina answered as the gun was entered into evidence. I tried to hold it together but as soon as I saw the gun I began crying uncontrollably. Smalls did his best to console me but it was to no avail, so he just held me and let me cry. Bazil stood up and the Bailiff stood up right along with him. Troy touched Bazil to get him to sit back down.

"Who's fingerprints were on the gun?"

"The defendant's fingerprints were on the gun."

"What happened next?"

"The Coroner took the bodies to the morgue, the officers continued to process the crime scene, and I left to go the hospital."

"Your Honor – may I share the crime scene photos with the jury?"

"Bailiff – please share the crime scene photos with the jury..." Judge Duffey ordered.

The Bailiff took a copy of the photos and shared them with the jury. Smalls continued to hold me as I cried. After the jury finished looking at the photos, the Bailiff took the copies and gave them back to Beverly...

"Detective – what happened when you got to the hospital?"

"I saw the defendant's neighbor, Keisha Cochran, and I asked her if I could get a statement.

"Was she cooperative?"

"Yes she was."

"Were you ever able to question her husband?"

"Yes."

"In your opinion – do you believe their statements are truthful?"

"Hole up – don't be calling me a liar!" Keisha blurted out from the back of the court room...

"Order in the court!" Judge Duffey snapped. "I will not tolerate outbursts from anyone in this court – unless you are called to the witness stand – you are to be quiet!"

"Sorry Your Honor..." Keisha said.

"Yes – I believe their statements are truthful..." Detective Jones answered.

"Were you able to get a statement from the defendant?"

"No – she refused to speak to me without her attorney..."

"Hmmmmm… I'm not surprised…"

"Objection!" Smalls yelled…

"Sustained…" Judge Duffey acknowledged.

"Your witness…" Beverly said as she sat down…

"Are you okay?" Smalls asked me…

"No…"

"I'll be right here…"

"I know…" I said as he went up to the stand…

"Hello Katina…"

"Good morning…"

"You testified the defendant pushed you – is that correct?"

"Objection – asked and answered!" Beverly snapped.

"Smalls – are you going somewhere?" Judge Duffey asked…

"Yes Your Honor…"

"I'll allow it – objection overruled…" Judge Duffey ordered…

"You could have placed the defendant under arrest at that moment – but you didn't – why?"

"I knew she wasn't going anywhere…"

"So – to be clear – you knew she wasn't running?"

"Yes."

"You testified that you were able to get a statement from the neighbors – and you also testified that you believed their statements were truthful – is that correct?"

"Yes."

"Your Honor – may I share the neighbor's statements with the jury?"

"Bailiff – please share the statements with the jury..." Judge Duffey ordered. The Bailiff used a projector to put their statements on screen. The statements were clear and legible to the jury. The judge allowed the jury a few minutes to read the statements before Smalls continued...

"Is it true that you bagged and tagged their neighbor, Keisha Cochran's clothes into evidence?"

"Yes."

"Did you find blood on the clothes?"

"Yes."

"Who did the blood belong to?"

"The blood belonged to Bazil Osgood, Sonia Santos, and Trevor Joseph."

"You testified you were in the bedroom of the defendant's home – is that correct?"

"Yes."

"You also testified that the officers continued to process the crime scene – is that correct?"

"Yes."

"To your knowledge – is there a bathroom in the defendant's bedroom?"

"Yes – there is."

"What - if anything – was recovered from the bathroom?"

"DNA was recovered that matched the defendant as well as her husband."

"Could you be more specific?'"

"We recovered semen matching Bazil Osgood and hair matching the defendant and Bazil Osgood."

"Did you recover any blood?"

"No we did not."

"So – to be clear – my client has been charged with the attempted murder of her husband – the murder of Sonia Santos – the murder of Trevor Joseph – my client had blood on her from her husband as well as the other victims – they have a master bathroom – and you didn't recover a single drop of blood from the bathroom?"

"No we did not."

"So – based on your testimony – my client did not try and take a shower to wash away evidence – instead – she ran outside to jump in the ambulance with her husband – is that correct?"

"That's correct."

"Hmmmmm - thank you – I have no further questions…" Smalls said with a smile as he sat down. "You okay?" Smalls whispered to me. I didn't answer – I just shook my head no…

"Court's in recess – be back in 15 minutes…" Judge Duffey said as he stood up and left the bench. The Bailiff escorted the jurors to the waiting room and Troy, Keisha, and Bazil went out into the hallway.

"C'mon..." Smalls said as he got up and waited for me. He took me by the hand, and we walked out into the hallway...

"Beautiee..." Bazil said as he pulled me into his arms. The Bailiffs were going to object but once we started crying they just stood there watching. Troy, Keisha, and Smalls hugged us both as we held each other and cried...

"We gotchall..." Troy said as he started crying...

"Don't start that shit Troy..." Keisha sniffed...

"This some bullshit!" Troy snapped...

"I know – shit – here comes the Bailiff..." Smalls said. The Bailiff walked towards us, stopped to observe, then went towards the men's room...

"I love the song..." Bazil said before he pulled me into a kiss...

"And I love you..." I said before I kissed him back...

"Promise me you'll sing it to me when you get home..." he breathed before he kissed me again...

"I promise..." I said as we continued kissing...

"Ahem!" The Bailiff interrupted. We all turned around to look at the Bailiff. "Judge Duffey's waiting…" he said.

"Oh okay – let's go…" Smalls said as he took my hand and pulled me into the court room and up to the table. Bazil, Troy, and Keisha came into the court room and sat down in the back.

"All rise…"the Bailiff said. Everyone stood up. "Department One of the Superior Court is now in session. Judge Duffey presiding. Please be seated."

"Calling the case of the People of the State of Connecticut versus Beautiee Osgood. Are both sides ready?"

"Ready for the People, Your Honor…" Beverly said.

"Ready for the Defense, Your Honor…" Smalls said.

"Beverly – are you ready to call your next witness?" Judge Duffey asked.

"Yes Your Honor."

"Very well – you may call your next witness…"

"Thank you Your Honor – I call Beautiee Osgood."

"Please state your name for the record…" Judge Duffey instructed…

"Beautiee Osgood."

"Please raise your right hand and place your left hand on the bible…" Judge Duffey

86

instructed as the court clerk held the bible... "Do you swear, under penalty of perjury, that the testimony you are about to give shall be the truth, the whole truth, and nothing but the truth?"

"I will..." I said as I sat down.

"Very well – Beverly – you may proceed..."

"Mrs. Osgood – please tell the court what happened on the night of January 13, 2019..."

"I invited Sonia Santos over."

"Why did you invite Sonia over?"

"You already know why she was invited over."

"Your Honor – Permission to Treat The Witness Hostile!" Beverly snapped!

"Permission granted – you may proceed..." Judge Duffey acknowledged...

"Mrs. Osgood – I'm going to ask you again..." she said as she walked up to the bench to get closer to my face... "WHY DID YOU INVITE SONIA SANTOS TO YOUR HOME?" I started waiving my hand to shoo her away from me. Smalls was shaking his head no but I didn't care...

"Could you back up please?" I asked sarcastically...

"Your Honor!" Beverly snapped before she was interrupted...

"Mrs. Osgood – answer the question!" Judge Duffey snapped...

"Your Honor – I have no problem answering questions – but she needs to back up – her breath stinks!" Everyone bust out laughing and Judge Duffey was not amused… "Order in the fucking court – now! Mrs. Osgood – let me warn you – today is not the day to test me – do I make myself clear?"

"Yes Your Honor – I meant no disrespect – I'm sorry…" I said as I put my head down…

"I'm not the one you need to apologize too…" Judge Duffey said as he pointed to Beverly…

"I'm sorry – I didn't mean to offend you…" I lied…

"Apology accepted – please answer the question…" she said as she backed up. I could see she was pissed off and I knew I had her where I wanted her…

"I invited Sonia over to have sex with me while my husband watched." The jurors gasped. Troy and Keisha had their mouths open in shock.

"And Sonia agreed to this?"

"Yes."

"You're lying right now – aren't you?" I could see the anger was building in her. Smalls looked at me pleading with his eyes not to lose my cool – but I knew what I was doing…

"I'm not lying…"

"You really expect the court to believe you invited Sonia over to have sex with you – and she knew your husband was in the closet – and she was okay with that?"

"Yes."

"Hmmmmm – too bad we can't ask Sonia – isn't it?"

"Objection…" Smalls said.

"Sustained…" Judge Duffey acknowledged…

"Did your husband participate?"

"Yes he did."

"And it was consensual?"

"Yes it was."

"You're lying – it wasn't consensual at all – you set your husband up so you could kill him…"

"Stop it! That's not true!" Bazil yelled…

"Bailiff – remove him from the court room – now!" Judge Duffey ordered. Bazil got up and left the court room before the Bailiff could reach him, but he stood outside so he could continue listening. The Bailiff stood in the back of the court room to make sure Bazil didn't come back in as Beverly continued…

"How did Trevor get in your house?"

"I don't know."

"Isn't it true that you invited him?"

"No I didn't."

"Would you change your answer if I told you we have surveillance of Trevor, in fact, letting himself in and not breaking in?"

"My answer wouldn't change – I didn't invite Trevor to my home."

"What happened – in your words?"

"Sonia agreed to come to the house. We had some wine, we went upstairs to the bedroom, and we started having sex."

"Where was your husband?"

"He was in the closet watching."

"Did he stay in the closet?"

"No."

"So he came out the closet – then what happened?"

"He had sex with me."

"Hmmmmm – interesting – so you had no idea that Trevor was in the closet?"

"No."

"When did you realize Trevor was in the closet?"

"When I was on my back."

"On your back?"

"Yes – I was on my back on the bed."

"And where was Sonia?"

"She was on top of me."

"Hmmmmm – and where was your husband?"

"He was on my right side."

"And he didn't know Trevor was in the closet?"

"No."

"Okay – so when did you see Trevor?"

"I saw the gun first – I screamed for Bazil to watch out..." I said as I started to cry... "But

Bazil didn't move fast enough... Oh God!" I cried...

"Is that when your husband was shot?"

"Yes..."

"What happened next?"

"I realized it was Trevor when he stepped out of the closet... he pointed the gun... I thought he was pointing it at both of us so I pulled Sonia down on top of me... Sonia got shot in the back – Trevor dropped the gun – he said it was all my fault – he said Sonia didn't deserve to die – he pulled Sonia off me and hugged her – I picked up the gun – and I shot him!" I cried. The jurors gasped...

"So – let me get this straight – are you telling us that Trevor let himself in your house – snuck in your closet with a gun – shot your husband – shot Sonia – dropped the gun – blamed you for it all – and then pulled Sonia off of you – instead of finishing the job and shooting you too?"

"Yeeesss!" I cried...

"Nice try Mrs. Osgood – but the truth is you invited Trevor to your home along with Sonia – you got them to let their guard down – you shot your husband – you shot Sonia – and you shot Trevor too – isn't that what really happened? Isn't it?"

"Noooo...." I cried...

"I have no further questions!" Beverly said as she sat down… "Your witness!" she said as she flung up her hands…

"Your Honor – may I be excused to get my client some water?" Smalls asked….

"No you may not be excused – if your client needs some water the Bailiff can get it – please continue…" Judge Duffey ordered…

"Yes Your Honor – Beautiee – are you okay to continue?"

"Yes…"

"Did you shoot your husband?"

"Noooo…." I cried…

"Did you shoot Sonia?"

"Nooo…"

"Did you shoot Trevor?"

"Yes…"

"Why?"

"Because he shot Bazil and he was going to shoot me…"

"Is it your testimony that you believe Trevor was going to shoot you if you didn't shoot him?"

"Yes…."

"Did you invite Trevor to your house?"

"No!" I cried.

"No further questions…" Smalls said as he sat back down…

"Courts in recess – we're closed for lunch – everyone be back at 1pm sharp!" Judge Duffey snapped before he stood up and left the bench.

Smalls got up from the table and I got up to follow him out the court room. Troy and Keisha were already in the hall with Bazil when we got there...

"Bazil..." I cried as I fell into his arms...

"Break it up..." the Bailiff ordered – but we ignored him.

"My client isn't doing anything wrong – leave her alone..." Smalls said as he stood in front of us...

"Either they break it up – or I make sure Judge Duffey has you removed as counsel!" the Bailiff growled...

"I'll go..." Bazil said as he let me go...

"You can't leave – you're up after lunch..."

"Excuse me?" Smalls asked.

"Check your witness list – he's up after lunch..." the Bailiff said. Smalls checked his list and saw the Bailiff was correct. "That's why I told y'all to break it up – you can't conversate before you give testimony..."

"You could'a just told me that!" Smalls snapped.

"You're right – I could've – see you at 1pm sharp..." he laughed as we walked off...

"Yo – that shit right there – mutha fucka!" Troy yelled...

"Troy – keep it down..." Keisha said...

"Fuck him!" Troy snapped...

"I know – but Beautiee needs us right now – we can't afford to lose it – she can't afford it…" Smalls said…

"Fuck this – yo Bazil – let's go outside a minute…" Troy said as he stormed off…

"Don't mind him – he gets like that when someone he cares about is being mistreated…" Keisha explained.

"I know – I love y'all…" I said…

"We love you too…Shit – where the hell did Troy go – oh that's him calling me – bye y'all – she said as she left…

"C'mon…" Smalls said as he took me to the attorney-client room… "Sit down…" he said as I sat down and then he sat down across from me… "Le'me ask you something – and be honest…"

"Okay…"

"Did Beverly's breath really stink?"

"A little…"

"Oh shit…" he laughed… "You were serious?"

"I said that to piss her off… and it worked…"

"Whhaaattt?"

"I did it on purpose… she played right into my hands… and the jury bought it… hook, line, and sinker!" I laughed as I banged my hand on the table…

"Beautiee… did you lie?"

"Smalls?"

"Yes?"

"Do you really believe I lied on the stand?"

"No... at least I don't want to believe that... but..."

"But Beverly is the Bitch that's trying to put me away – I didn't lie – all I did – all she did – was show the jury who she really is..."

"You hungry?"

"Yea..."

"Okay – I'ma go get us some lunch – I'll be right back – please – whatever you do – don't leave this room!"

"Alright, alright!" I said as he ran out to get us lunch...

"Shit – I gotta pee – I'ma go to the bathroom right quick..."

"Hey Smalls – where's Beautiee?" Bazil asked when he saw Smalls walk inside the restaurant...

"She's waiting for me in the attorney-client conference room..." he answered as he picked up a menu...

"I'ma go holla at her right quick before everyone gets back..." Bazil said as he hurried towards the door...

"Don't get caught!" Smalls yelled... but Bazil was already across the street...

"Is that door opened?" Bazil heard the Bailiff ask someone as he went to the end of the hallway...

"Yea – it's still open…" they answered. Bazil hid in the corner so nobody would see him. He watched and waited for the Bailiff to come out. When he saw the Bailiff didn't lock the door, he hurried down to the attorney-client waiting room to look for me but I was still in the bathroom so he hurried down the hall and waited…

Chapter 9

"Beautiee!" Bazil whispered as he stuck his head out the door. I looked to the left then to the right... "Over here!" I turned around and saw him sticking his head out a door at the end of the hallway and I ran towards him. When I got to the door, Bazil snatched me inside, closed the door, and locked it...

"Where are we?" I whispered...

"We're in Judge Duffey's old chambers..." he answered as he started kissing me on my neck...

"Bazil..." I moaned...

"Ssshhhh..." he said before he pulled my face to his and forced his tongue in my mouth. We continued kissing feverishly as Bazil unzipped my prison jumpsuit and slid it off my shoulders...

"Beautiee – somebody's coming!" Bazil breathed as he helped me put my jumpsuit back on...

"Open this door – now!" the Bailiff yelled from the other side of the door...

"I'm coming!" I answered as Bazil dipped into the private bathroom. Once I saw he was in the bathroom I unlocked the door and opened it...

"You had no business in here – you know that – right?" the Bailiff asked as he snatched me by the arm...

"Yes..." I answered...

"Let's go – Judge Duffey already told you he doesn't like to be kept waiting..." he said as he pulled me out the judge's chambers and down the hall to the court room. Once I got inside the court room and I was seated next to Smalls, Bazil came into the court room and sat in the back.

"Where the hell were you?" Smalls whispered...

"I was with Bazil..." I whispered as I smiled...

"All rise..."the Bailiff said. Everyone stood up. "Department One of the Superior Court is now in session. Judge Duffey presiding. Please be seated."

"Calling the case of the People of the State of Connecticut versus Beautiee Osgood. Are both sides ready?"

"Ready for the People, Your Honor..." Beverly said.

"Ready for the Defense, Your Honor..." Smalls said.

"Beverly – you may call your next witness..." Judge Duffey said...

"Thank you Your Honor – I call Bazil Osgood." The jurors gasped. Everyone else was quiet. Bazil stood up, adjusted himself, and walked up to the stand...

"Please state your name for the record..." Judge Duffey instructed...

"Bazil Osgood."

"Please raise your right hand and place your left hand on the bible..." Judge Duffey instructed as the court clerk held the Bible... "Do you swear, under penalty of perjury, that the testimony you are about to give shall be the truth, the whole truth, and nothing but the truth?"

"Absolutely..." Bazil said as he sat down.

"Very well – Beverly – you may proceed..."

"Good afternoon Mr. Osgood..."

"Hello..."

"Do you remember what happened to you on January 13, 2019?"

"I don't remember everything..."

"What do you remember?"

"I remember Sonia was having sex with my wife, I remember joining in... and then I got shot..."

"Are you sure that's what you remember?"

"I remember that..."

'Your Honor – permission to treat the witness as hostile!"

"Permission granted – continue..." Judge Duffey ordered.

"Mr. Osgood – isn't it true that you're merely repeating what your wife told you?"

"Some of it – yes…"

"How can you be sure what she told you is true?"

"My wife loves me – she wouldn't lie about that…" I started crying and Smalls grabbed my hand under the table…

"Is that right?"

"Yes…"

"So – your wife slept with your lover – stabbed you – and left you – but she wouldn't lie to you? Really?"

"My wife loves me – she wouldn't lie to me…"

"Mr. Osgood – I know you love your wife – but you also loved Trevor – isn't that true?"

"Yes…"

"And – based on your wife's testimony – he betrayed you by sleeping with your wife – and – based on your wife's testimony – he shot you – but you loved him – so how can you be sure you wife's telling you the truth?"

"I just am…"

"Mr. Osgood – you've been betrayed by the two people you love most – and yet – you continue to stand by your wife – and she doesn't deserve it…"

"She does!" Bazil snapped as Beverly turned around. Smalls looked at me and grabbed my hand harder to remind me to remain calm but it wasn't working...

"Does she? What did your wife do to earn your devotion?"

"She stayed with me every night I was in a coma – she never left my side..."

"Of course she did - she didn't do that for you – she did that for herself..."

"She made love to me..."

"Oh please – that just means she was horny!" Beverly laughed. Bazil started breathing heavy. His shoulders and his chest started going up and down. His eyes turned to slits... and I was scared. The jury watched and waited...

"When I came out my coma, my wife was there. We made love... and then I died..." Bazil said as he started crying...

"Oh Bazil..." I cried. Smalls pulled me into a hug. The jury was quiet. Troy and Keisha moved closer to the bench...

"You died?" Beverly asked...

"Yes."

"I'm sorry Mr. Osgood – I truly am – but I have to ask – how does this prove your wife loves you?"

"Because... after I died... my wife died..."

"Oh my God!" Keisha said out loud before covering her mouth. The jurors started whispering...

"Your wife died? After you did? How could you possibly know this?"

"Because she followed me…"

"Your wife followed you? Followed you where?"

"My wife followed me to the light…"

"Mr. Osgood – are you sure this wasn't a dream?"

"Yes."

"Okay – I'll entertain you – so your wife followed you to the light – what happened next?"

"I told her to go back but she wouldn't leave me…" he cried. I was crying and I could hear Troy and Keisha crying with me. Smalls was tearing up and so were the jurors…

"Let me get this straight – you died – your wife died – and she followed you?"

"Yes."

"What happened next Mr. Osgood?"

"We saw God…"

"You saw God? Both of you?"

"Yes."

"What happened next?"

"Beautiee begged for my life…" Bazil cried as we all continued crying.

"Your wife begged for your life? Hmmmmm – interesting – continue…"

"God told Beautiee to trust him so she let me go…"

"So - Mr. Osgood – if – as you say – your wife let you go – how are you here?"

"I begged God please don't make Beautiee live without me!" he cried. I saw that Judge Duffey was getting emotional too.

"Mr. Osgood – are you telling the court you asked God to let you come back to your wife – and that's why you're here?"

"Yes..."

"Mr.Osgood – you're an intelligent man – right?"

"Yes..."

"So – let me ask you – isn't it possible that you're here because the doctor revived you?"

"Of course..."

"You love your wife very much – don't you?"

"Yes..."

"You'd do anything to protect her – right?"

"Yes..."

"I have one last question - if it was a matter of life and death – would you lie for her? Bazil didn't answer right away. Everyone waited for him to answer...

"Yes..."

"I have no further questions – your witness..." Beverly said as she sat down.

"Hey Bazil..." Smalls said as he stood up...

"Hey Smalls..." Bazil said as he smiled.

"You testified that you don't remember everything that happened the night you were shot – right?"

"Yes."

"You also testified you loved Trevor – is that right?"

"Yes."

"Did you ever cut things off with Trevor?"

"Yes."

"How did he feel about that?"

"He begged me not to."

"Did he say why?"

"He begged me not to let my wife come between us..." Keisha and Troy gasped along with the jury.

"But you ended it anyway – didin't you?"

"Yes..."

"Why?"

"Because I didn't want to hurt my wife anymore..." he cried...

"Did that make Trevor angry?"

"I'm not sure..."

"Let me re-phrase the question – isn't it possible that Trevor was angry – just like your wife was angry when she found out about him?"

"Yes... it's possible..."

"So... isn't it also possible that your wife was telling you the truth when she told you that Trevor shot you, shot Sonia, and would have also shot her if she didn't shoot him?"

"It's absolutely possible..."

"Thank you – I have no further questions..." Smalls said as he sat down.

"Please return to the back of the court room..." Judge Duffey said. Bazil got up and went to the back of the court room. Troy and Keisha got up and went to the back of the court room to sit with him.

"Beverly – are you ready to call your next witness?" Judge Duffey asked...

"Yes Your Honor – I call Dr. Ronald Preston." Bazil and I smiled as we watched Dr. Preston took the stand...

"Please state your name for the record..." Judge Duffey instructed...

"Ronald Preston."

"Please raise your right hand and place your left hand on the bible..." Judge Duffey instructed as the court clerk held the Bible... "Do you swear, under penalty of perjury, that the testimony you are about to give shall be the truth, the whole truth, and nothing but the truth?"

"I swear..." Dr. Preston said as he sat down.

"Very well – Beverly – you may proceed..."

"Dr. Preston – what happened on the night Mr. Osgood was brought into the hospital?"

"Mr. Osgood needed emergency surgery. I had to struggle to get the bullet out of him. The surgery went well but when I went to close him up he started coding. His pressure kept dropping so I told him I was trying to get him back to his wife but I needed him to cooperate and relax."

"Do you always talk to your patients when their unconscious?"

"I started talking to my patients after my mother told me she heard everything that was said to her when she was in a coma."

"Go on…"

"I went to see Mrs. Osgood and let her know what happened with her husband during surgery. I explained to her that we had to put him in a medical coma because he lost a lot of blood, his pressure was low, and he was too weak to heal. I didn't think he was going to make it at the time – she asked me what should she do and I told her if she believed in God – she should pray."

"Oh my God!" Troy said. I was crying, Bazil was crying, and Smalls was tearing up along with some of the jurors.

"What happened next?"

"I asked Mrs. Osgood why she was naked."

"What was her response?"

"She said she was having sex with her husband when he got shot. I asked her why she didn't get dressed and she said there wasn't any time, so I asked one of my nurses to get her some pajamas and let her take a shower."

"Was the defendant there every night as Mr. Osgood testified?"

"Yes she was. I've seen a lot of patients with their families and loved ones and I've never seen more dedication and devotion to a patient like I saw with Mrs. Osgood – he's a lucky man." Smalls smiled as Beverly got annoyed…

"Dr. Preston – Mr. Osgood testified that he woke up from his comma – he died – the defendant died – they both saw God – she came back – and he came back – is this true?"

"I can't tell you what happened between them and God because I wasn't there – but what I can tell you is that he died – I tried to revive him but I failed – she died – I was able to revive her – and then he woke up on his own."

"Are you saying you believe they saw God?"

"I'm saying there must be a God because there's no other possible medical explanation for what happened..." Dr. Preston said as he threw up his hands...

"I have no more questions... your witness..." Beverly said as she sat down and shook her head...

"I have no questions for this witness Your Honor..." Smalls said.

"The witness is excused – we're done for today – I'll see everyone tomorrow morning at 9 a.m." Judge Duffey said as he got up from the bench and left. Everyone left the court room except me and Smalls...

"You ready?" Smalls asked...

"No..." I said as I started to cry...

"I know... it's almost over... Bazil's waiting..." he said as he got up to take my hand...

"Okay…" I said as I got up and he walked me into the hallway. Bazil grabbed me as soon as I came out the court room…

"Beautiee… we need to go…" Smalls said as he tugged my arm…"

"Just a few more minutes… please…" I pleaded. Bazil picked up my face and kissed me fully.

"I'll see you tomorrow…" he said before he let me go and left the court house. The Bailiff came over to escort me back to the waiting area with the other prisoners…

"I'll see you first thing tomorrow morning…" Smalls said as he pulled me into a hug…

"Okay…" I sighed…

"Let's go…" the Bailiff said as he took me by the arm. I watched Smalls leave the court house…

"We'll be back tomorrow…" Troy said as Troy and Keisha hugged me together…

"I love y'all…" I said…

"We love you too…" Keisha said before they let me go and then they left the court house. The Bailiff escorted me back to the waiting area to go back to jail.

Chapter 10

"All rise..."the Bailiff said. Everyone stood up. "Department One of the Superior Court is now in session. Judge Duffey presiding. Please be seated."

"Calling the case of the People of the State of Connecticut versus Beautiee Osgood. Are both sides ready?"

"Ready for the People, Your Honor..." Beverly said.

"Ready for the Defense, Your Honor..." Smalls said.

"Beverly – you may call your next witness..." Judge Duffey said...
"Thank you Your Honor – I call Tisha Andrews."
I watched as Ms. Andrews took the stand...

"Please state your name for the record..." Judge Duffey instructed...

"Tisha Andrews."

"Please raise your right hand and place your left hand on the bible…" Judge Duffey instructed as the court clerk held the Bible… "Do you swear, under penalty of perjury, that the testimony you are about to give shall be the truth, the whole truth, and nothing but the truth?"

"I do…" Tisha said as she sat down.

"Ms. Andrews – please tell the court what happened on January 13, 2019 when the defendant came into the hospital…"

"Mrs. Osgood was distraught. She was covered in blood. She had a robe on but it kept opening. She didn't seem to care that everyone could see her naked body."

"Did you find that odd?"

"Yes I did. I thought it was strange that she didn't take a shower or have clothes on."

"Did you have a conversation with the defendant?"

"Yes I did."

"What did you discuss?"

"I explained to Mrs. Osgood that we needed to do a rape kit, take some pictures, and take some samples."

"How did she react?"

"Mrs. Osgood was angry – she refused to allow me or anyone else to do a rape kit."

"Did you find that odd?"

"Yes I did – if we were able to do a rape kit – we could've determined that she only had sex with her husband and no one else."

"Did you explain that to the defendant?"

"No – I only explained we needed to do a rape kit as a procedure due to the circumstances."

"Did the defendant do a rape kit?"

"No – she refused – she said she wasn't raped."

"I see – were you able to get photos and samples?"

"Yes."

"Your Honor – may I share the photos with the jury?"

"Objection!" Smalls yelled…

"What's your objection Smalls?" Judge Duffey asked…

"Why is it necessary for the jury to see photos of my client naked?"

"Due to the heinous nature of the crimes – I'm sorry – your objection is overruled – Bailiff – please share the photos with the jury." I sat there numb. All I could do was cry. Smalls put his arm around me to comfort me…

"I'm sorry…" he whispered. I watched as the Bailiff passed the photos to the jury – thankfully they weren't too interested – some of the jurors even waived their hand to let the Bailiff know they didn't want to see them. Beverly continued with her questions after the Bailiff returned the photos…

"What was your opinion as you were taking the photos and getting swabs from the defendant?"

"I told Mrs. Osgood I thought she was an angry black woman that shot her husband because she caught him cheating on her…"

"Oh Shit!" Troy said out loud. The jury gasped…

"Thank you – your witness…" Beverly said to Smalls as she sat down…

"Ms. Andrews – you testified that you found it odd that the defendant's robe kept opening – why did you find that odd when you also testified that she appeared to be distraught?"

"People don't normally come to the hospital without getting dressed…"

"Are you comparing the situation with my client to visitors?"

"No… I'm just saying…"

"You're saying that instead of my client staying with her husband because she was afraid he might die – that she should've thought more about taking a shower and getting dressed?"

"Objection – he's badgering the witness!" Beverly snapped…

"Sustained…" Judge Duffey acknowledged…

"Sorry Your Honor – Ms. Andrews – why did you insist on a rape kit when the defendant told you she wasn't raped?"

"As I stated – its procedure in situations like this – it wasn't personal…"

"Isn't it true that rape kits are only procedure when someone says they've been raped?"

"Normally – yes – but nothing about this was normal!"

"Exactly – you also testified that you told the defendant you thought she was an angry black woman that shot her husband because she caught him cheating on her – what made you think that?"

"Because she was covered in blood…"

"Isn't it possible that the defendant was covered in blood due to blood splatter?"

"Yes it is…"

"Isn't it also possible that the blood could've gotten on the defendant because she held her husband close to her?"

"Yes – it's possible…"

"It's not just possible – it's probable – no further questions…" Smalls said as he sat down…

"Beverly – you may call your next witness…" Judge Duffey ordered…

"Thank you Your Honor – I call Mr. A. Grady – the Coroner from the Fairfield County Medical Examiner's Office.

"Please state your name for the record…" Judge Duffey instructed…

"Mr. A. Grady."

"Please raise your right hand and place your left hand on the bible..." Judge Duffey instructed as the court clerk held the Bible... "Do you swear, under penalty of perjury, that the testimony you are about to give shall be the truth, the whole truth, and nothing but the truth?"

"I do..." Mr. Grady said as he sat down.

"Mr. Grady – on January 13, 2019 – did you perform the autopsies on Sonia Santos and Trevor Joseph?"

"Yes I did."

"Please tell the court what you determined to be the cause of death during the autopsies..."

"The cause of death for Sonia Santos was a single shot in the back under the right shoulder blade. The cause of death for Trevor Joseph was a single shot to the chest. Both victims were shot within close range."

"How were you able to determine this?"

"I was able to determine that by the depth of the bullet penetration into each of the bodies."

"Could you please explain?"

"We take two radiographs at 90 degrees to each other to estimate the depth of the bullet in the body. Once we determine the depth of the bullet into the body, we place bullets of different calibers alongside the body at a suitable position and then image them to compare the bullet caliber."

"Did you examine the bullet removed from Mr. Osgood?"

"Yes I did."

"What did you find?"

"The bullet removed from Mr. Osgood was a perfect match to the bullets removed from Sonia Santos and Trevor Joseph."

"Thank you – your witness..." Beverly said to Smalls as she sat down...

"Mr. Grady..." Smalls asked as he stood up... "You testified that both Sonia Santos and Trevor Joseph were shot in close range – is that correct?"

"Yes."

"And you testified that Sonia Santos was shot in the back – right?"

"Yes."

"In your opinion – if both victims were close to the defendant – wouldn't one of them have jumped to the side to avoid being shot?"

"Not necessarily..."

"Please explain..."

"Well – if the defendant had the gun pointed at them and told them not to move – they might not have moved – it's possible the defendant may have told them to put their hands up and don't move..."

"Mr. Grady – do you see the defendant here in the court room?"

"Yes."

"And do you also see the defendant's husband in the court room?"

"Yes I do."

"And – since you performed the autopsies – both Sonia Santos and Trevor Joseph are taller and larger than the defendant – right?"

"Yes."

"So – do you really think it's possible that my client held her husband – held Sonia – and held Trevor – at gun point – then shot all three of them – and they just stood there with their hands up – without a struggle – and no one tried to get the gun away from her?" The Coroner hesitated before answering...

"Well... since you put it that way... no..." The jurors started whispering. Bazil and I smiled.

"Thank you – no further questions..." Smalls said as he sat down.

"The witness is excused." Judge Duffy waited for Mr. Grady to leave the stand before continuing... "Does the prosecution rest?"

"Yes Your Honor..." Beverly answered.

"Does the defense rest?"

"Yes Your Honor..." Smalls answered.

"Are you ready with final arguments?" Judge Duffey asked...

"Yes Your Honor..." Beverly answered.

"Yes Hour Honor..." Smalls answered.

"Very well – you may begin..." Judge Duffey said. Beverly went first...

Chapter 11

Beverly's Closing Argument

"Ladies and gentlemen of the jury,

You've heard a lot of testimony. You've seen a lot of evidence. As you go into deliberations, I want you to remember the defendant's testimony. She testified she caught her husband cheating on her. She testified she slept with her husband's lover to hurt him. She testified she stabbed him. She testified she left him. She testified she invited Sonia Santos over for her husband to watch them have sex and later join in – but the truth is – she set them both up along with Trevor Joseph. She testified she didn't invite Trevor into their home – but how can we believe that when she slept with him? And yes – we've seen a lot of affection between these two – but don't believe for one second that the defendant love's her husband – he definitely love's her – but she doesn't love anyone but herself – she's doing what she does – whatever it takes to protect her own interests. The defendant had reason, motive, and opportunity to get them all – and she executed it perfectly – well... almost perfectly. When you're done with your deliberations – return with a verdict of 'Guilty' on all counts. Thank you."

Small's Closing Argument

"Ladies and gentlemen of the jury,

I agree with the prosecution – you should remember the defendant's testimony. Yes – she did testify that her husband cheated on her – and yes – she testified she slept with her husband's lover to hurt him – because she was hurt. Yes ˗ she did testify she stabbed her husband – in his hand! If she were trying to kill her husband – she would have stabbed in in the heart, the chest, the neck – even his back! No one has ever died from being stabbed in the hand! Yes – she also testified she left him – again – if she wanted to kill him – he wouldn't have been able to walk out the house before she left! Yes – she testified she invited Sonia Santos over for her husband to watch them have sex and later join in – since when is having a threesome a crime? In spite of what the prosecution wants you to think – Trevor Joseph was not invited to their home. Yes – the defendant slept with him – but that is not an invitation to come over and the prosecution didn't prove otherwise! And yes – we've all witnessed the genuine affection between the defendant and her husband. I have no doubt whatsoever that the love between them is real – and neither should you. The prosecution would have you believe the defendant had reason – yes she did have reason – she had reason to leave her husband – and she left her husband – but she went back to her husband because she loves her husband – she didn't go back to her husband to kill him! And yes – the defendant had reason and motive to invite Sonia Santos over to their home – and that reason and motive was sex – not murder – and remember – according to the Coroner's testimony – Sonia was shot in the back – how was the defendant able to shoot her husband – then turn around and shoot Sonia in the back unless Sonia turned her back on the defendant – and – if the defendant was responsible for the gun – once she shot her husband – neither Sonia nor Trevor would turn their back on the defendant – let alone stand still and wait to be shot! My client has been through too much already. When you're done with your deliberations – return with a verdict of 'Not Guilty' on all counts. Thank you."

"Ladies and gentlemen of the jury, I am now going to read to you the law that you must follow in deciding this case…" Judge Duffey said as he stood up and began reading…

1. COURT'S STANDARD INSTRUCTIONS TO THE JURY IN A CRIMINAL TRIAL

"It is my duty to instruct you on the rules of law that you must use in deciding this case. After I've completed these instructions, you will go to the jury room and begin your discussions or what we call your deliberations in this case. You must decide whether the Government has proved beyond a reasonable doubt the specific facts necessary to find the Defendant guilty of the crimes charged in the indictment."

Judge Duffey continued to instruct the jury on the following:

2. DUTY TO FOLLOW INSTRUCTIONS PRESUMPTION OF INNOCENCE

3. DEFINITION OF REASONABLE DOUBT

4. CONSIDERATION OF THE EVIDENCE, DIRECT AND CIRCUMSTANTIAL-- ARGUMENT OF COUNSEL COMMENTS BY THE COURT

5. CREDIBILITY OF WITNESSES

6. IMPEACHMENT INCONSISTENT STATEMENT

7. DEFENDANT TESTIFIES WITH NO FELONY CONVICTION

8. EXPERT WITNESSES

9. INTRODUCTION TO SPECIFIC OFFENSE INSTRUCTION

10. ON OR ABOUT

11. KNOWINGLY AND WILLFULLY AND SPECIFIC INTENT

12. CAUTION – PUNISHMENT (SINGLE DEFENDANT – MULTIPLE COUNTS)

13. DUTY TO DELIBERATE

14. FOREPERSON AND PROCEDURE

"These are your instructions. You will now go to the jury room but do not begin your deliberations until you receive the exhibits and I tell you that your deliberations may begin." We all sat there quiet, waiting for about an hour for the jury to decide my fate...

"We're ready..." Juror#2 said to the Court Security Officer. The Court Security Officer notified Judge Duffey as the Bailiff escorted the jurors back into the jury box. We all watched as the Bailiff handed the form to the court clerk. The court clerk stood up and began reading:

"On the Charge of Attempted Murder in the First Degree of Bazil Osgood – we, the jury, find the defendant...Not Guilty!"

"Yes!" Troy said behind us before putting his hand over his mouth. Smalls smiled, Bazil and I clung to each other, and Beverly shook her head...

"On the Charge of Murder in the First Degree of Sonia Santos – we, the jury, find the defendant... Not Guilty!"

"Thank you Lord..." Keisha whispered. Smalls looked over at Beverly, taunting her with an even bigger Smile, Bazil pulled me into a kiss, and Beverly sat down and folded her arms in defeat...

"On the Charge of Murder in the First Degree of Trevor Joseph – we, the jury, find the defendant...Guilty!" Beverly stood up from the table and looked directly as Smalls with a 'Finally Gotchu Mutha Fucka' look on her face.

Smalls shook his head, sighed, turned to me and whispered...

"I'm sorry..." Bazil and I clung to each other as tears streamed down our faces...

"Yo – that's fucked up..." Troy said as he choked up. Keisha pulled him into a hug as he started crying...

"Foreman of the Jury please stand..." Judge Duffey ordered. Male Juror #2 stood up...

"Is the verdict correct?"

"Yes your honor..." Male Juror #2 sighed...

"Bailiff – please give the attorney's an opportunity to examine the verdict form." Beverly examined the form first. She tried not to gloat as she held it in her hand but she couldn't contain her excitement. The Bailiff took the verdict form and brought it to Smalls. Smalls snatched the form, looked at it, and threw it down on the table. The Bailiff went to pick it up but Bazil snatched it up to read it before the Bailiff could...

"Bazil..." Smalls whispered as he touched Bazil's hand..."

"This isn't right... there must be some mistake..." Bazil cried... "Your Honor... please... take me..."

"Mr. Osgood... please give the form to the Bailiff..." Judge Duffey ordered. Bazil handed the form to the Bailiff, the Bailiff handed the form back to the court clerk, and then Judge Duffey spoke... "Very well..." he sighed...

"The jury is dismissed. Thank you for your service." The Bailiff opened the door to the waiting room and escorted the jury out the waiting room through another exit. When the Bailiff returned to the court room Judge Duffey spoke again... "Will the defendant, Beautiee Osgood, please rise." I stood up but my legs began to tremble. Bazil stood up and held on to me for dear life... "On the Charge of Attempted Murder in the First Degree of your husband – Bazil Osgood – you have been found Not Guilty. On the Charge of Murder in the First Degree of Sonia Santos – you have been found Not Guilty. On the Charge of Murder in the First Degree of Trevor Joseph – you have been found Guilty – however – based on the testimony – it is the opinion of this court that the prosecution failed to prove you had intention of killing Trevor Joseph with malice or contempt. It is also the opinion of this court that since your fingerprints were the only fingerprints on the gun and all three victims were shot by the same gun – you can't possibly be guilty of murdering one victim without also being guilty of murdering the other victim and attempting to murder your husband - therefore – I'm setting aside the Guilty Verdict and entering a judgement of acquittal..." he said and then he banged the gavel for emphasis. "Mrs. Osgood – you're free to go." Beverly threw up her hands and fell back in the chair. Smalls stood up, chest out, smiling, fighting back tears...

"Oh shit! That's what I'm talkin' about!" Troy said as he hugged Keisha and they jumped up and down. Bazil and I were kissing like nobody else was in the court room...

"Mrs. Osgood?" Judge Duffey interrupted...

"Yes Your Honor?"

"I said you're free to go..." he laughed...

"Oh – right..." I said as I let go of Bazil and ran to the bench...

"You're going the wrong way..." Judge Duffey laughed as he pointed in the opposite direction...

"Thank you..." I cried as I threw my arms around his neck and hugged him...

"Smalls – come get your client before I change my damn mind..." he laughed. I let go, ran back to Bazil, and jumped into his arms, knocking him down on the floor. Everyone bust out laughing...

"C'mon y'all..." Smalls laughed as he helped me up, and then Bazil...

"Let's go!" Bazil said as he snatched me by the hand and pulled me out the court room...

Chapter 12

"Where we goin'?" I asked... running to keep up...

"Follow me..." he said as he ran out the court house and I followed him across the street to the Holiday Inn...

"Mr. Osgood – nice to see you..." the clerk said as she put his card on the counter...

"You're all set..." she said as she handed Bazil the keys, he snatched my hand again, and pulled me towards the elevator. When the elevator doors opened, Bazil pulled me inside, pushed me against the back, and held his body against me as he kissed me. The bell rang, the door opened, and Bazil pulled me out the elevator and down the hall towards our room. When we got to our room, Bazil got the key, swiped it, opened the door, pulled me inside the room, and closed the door. Bazil continued kissing me as he unzipped the prison jumpsuit, slid it off my shoulders, and let it drop to the floor. I stood there and watched him take off his clothes until he was standing in front of me completely nude.

Bazil took me by the hand, led me into the bathroom, and turned on the shower. As the water got hot, he took my hand, led me into the shower, wrapped his arm around me, pulled me into a kiss, and held me against him as we continued kissing. I could feel his dick pressing against me so I reached down to grab it and started stroking it as Bazil reach down to play with my pussy. We continued kissing and playing with each other and moaned in each other's mouths as we came together...

"MmmmMmmm... MmmmMmmm..... MmmmMmmm..."
"Mmmmmph... Mmmmmph... Mmmmmph..."

Bazil soaped up the washcloth and washed me all over, taking his time on my breasts and between my legs. He turned me around and washed my back and my ass while pulling me close to him and kissing me on my neck. He turned me around to face him and I returned the favor, washing him all over, taking my time as he kissed me. When I reached his dick and his balls, I washed them with my hands and stroked him until he was hard again. I washed his back and his ass as Bazil pulled me closer and continued kissing me. Bazil turned off the water and led me out the shower. He stood me in front of the mirror so I could watch him dry me off while he stood in back of me, kissing me on my neck. When he finished drying me off, he dropped the towel, pushed me forward, spread my legs, and slid himself inside me.   I watched us in the mirror as he pulled me to him and began fucking me from behind...

"Oh Bazil..." I moaned as I braced myself on the counter and continued watching us in the mirror...

"Yes... Beautiee..." Bazil moaned as I watched him breathe in my ear and kiss my neck..."

"I'm cumming Bazil..." I moaned as I continued to watch us in the mirror...

"I'm cumming with you..." he moaned as I watched him grab my shoulders and I felt him fucking me harder...

"Bazil!!! I'm cummmmiiiinnnnggg!!!"

"Cum for me!!!" he growled as he fucked me harder and faster... and I saw my breasts swing back and forth in the mirror...

"Aaagggggghhhhhh!"

"Uuuugggghhhh!   Uuuuugggghhhhh! Uuuugggghhhhh!!!"

I continued watching us in the mirror as Bazil kissed me on my neck and shoulders until he turned me around to face him, pulled me close to him, and kissed me fully.   Bazil stopped kissing me, took me by the hand, and led me to bed. He turned back the covers and the sheets, climbed into bed, and I climbed in beside him, and lay on his chest as he wrapped his arm around me... and I started to cry...

"What's wrong... please don't cry..." Bazil whispered as he started crying with me...

"How could you still love me?" I cried...

"Beautiee..." he whispered before pulling me into a kiss... "How could you still love me?"

"After everything I've done..."

"Please..." he said as he kissed my tears... "I'm the one... it wasn't you... it was me..."

"I wish I never slept with Trevor..."

"I should've ended it as soon as I married you..."

"I should've just left you..."

"You did..."

"I mean... I never should've gone to the hotel..."

"Beautiee... please stop..." Bazil cried...

"I can't help it..."

"I've hurt you so much... I promised God I'd never hurt you again... and I broke that promise..." Bazil said as he cried even harder...

"No... my Thirst Quencher..." I whispered before pulling him into a kiss... "You've kept that promise..." I said before kissing him again... "Ever since you've come back to me... you haven't done anything to hurt me... please stop crying..." I said as I continued to cry...

"I'll stop if you will..." he said as we continued kissing...

"Okay..." I said as he pulled me close to him and pulled me down on the bed...

"Sing to me..." he said and then he started kissing me on my neck...

"Lovin' at first sight, lovin' me alright..." I sang...

"Yes... I love you..." Bazil breathed...

"Lovin' even when things ain't goin' right, Lovin' me all night 'till the mornin' light..."

"Love Me Baby..." Bazil sang with me...

"Lovin' me in spite of my many faults..." he sang as he touched my hair...

"Lovin' through the hurt, breakin' down my walls, Lovin' on my heart, kissin' all my scars..." I sang...

"Love Me Baby..." Bazil sang with me...

"Lovin' every day when I've lost my way..." he sang as we looked into each other's eyes... "Lovin' me is hard, don't know what to say..."

"Lovin' let's me know that you wanna stay..." I sang...

"Love Me Baby..." Bazil sang with me...

"Lovin' me in spite of it being hot..." he sang...

"Lovin' all the while even when I'm not..." I sang...

"Lovin' in the dark 'till you find the spot..."

"Love Me Baby..." we both sang...

"Lovin' how you touch, and I'm feelin' good..." I sang...

"Lovin' by my side like I knew you could..." he sang...

"Lovin' all along 'till I understood..." I sang...

"Love Me Baby..." we both sang. We melted into each other as Bazil pulled me closer, kissed me deeply, and we were making love again... until Bazil's cell phone rang...

"Yes Smalls..." Bazil answered without stopping...

"Yo – where the fuck are you?" Smalls asked...

"I'm... inside... Beautiee..." he breathed...

"I can't witchu – why'd you answer the phone?" he laughed...

"Because..." he breathed as I pulled him in deeper... "You wouldn't stop calling me... until I answered..."

"Hurry up... we're hungry..." Smalls laughed...

"Okay... we'll be there soon..." Bazil breathed as he dropped the phone on the floor...

"Is it time?" I breathed...

"Yes... it's time..."

"Okay..."

"We have to go..." he breathed and then he kissed me fully, covering my mouth with his while continuing to thrust deeper. I dug my fingers into the small of his back as my orgasm spread through my body and I started shaking. Bazil continued thrusting and came just as hard, kissing me so hard I nearly choked on his tongue...

"Hmmmmmph... Hmmmmmph... Hmmmmmpph..." I moaned, trying to catch my breath...

"Damn..." he breathed...

"I want more..."

"So do I..."

"Mmmmmm.... I don't wanna leave..." I breathed as we continued kissing...

"They're waiting... and they're hungry..."

"So am I..."

"I'll feed you again later..."

"Promise?"

"Promise..."

"Okay..." I sighed and got up out of bed...

"What's wrong?" Bazil asked as he watched me standing there shaking my head...

"I don't have anything to wear..."

"Check the closet..."

"Oh Bazil!" I cried when I saw the outfit from the night he proposed to me...

"Beautiee Osgood..." Bazil said as he got down on one knee and took my hand... "Will you marry me? Again?"

"Yes... my Thirst Quencher... yes..." I cried. Bazil took our wedding rings out the drawer to the end table and placed both rings on my finger. I took his ring, placed it on his finger, pulled Bazil's naked body close to me, and held him. "I love you so much my Thirst Quencher..." I said as tears streamed down my face...

"I love you too..." Bazil said as he pulled me into a kiss. "We better get dressed and get outta here..." he said as he dried my tears...

"Okay..." I sighed. We got dressed and started to leave when I stopped... "Bazil... wait a minute..."

"What's wrong?"

"Nothing..." I said as I picked up the prison jumpsuit off the floor...

"What are you doing with that?"

"I'm putting it where it belongs..." I answered as we left the room, closed the door, walked down the corridor, and I dropped it in the garbage can on our way to the lobby.

Chapter 13

"Surprise!" Everyone said as Bazil opened the door... and I burst into tears...

"Awww... Joselyn said as she started crying and hugged me..."

"I love y'all so much..." I cried...

"We love you too... stop crying..." Sam said as he fought back tears while hugging me...

"Stop crying man..." Bazil laughed as they hugged each other... "Thank you Joselyn..." Bazil said as he pulled Joselyn into a hug...

"What about me?" Sheila asked as she came over to us...

"What about you?" I laughed as we hugged each other...

"You don't need me to tell you how much I love you... but I'll tell you anyway... I love you..." Bazil said as he pulled her into a hug and kissed her on the cheek...

"Well... okay then..." Sheila blushed...

"Keisha..." I cried as we hugged each other...

"Stop cryin' – damn..." she laughed as she fought back tears...

"She's happy... and so am I..." Bazil said as he pulled Keisha into a hug...

"Bring it in man..." Troy said as he pulled Bazil away from his wife and hugged him...

"Smalls..." I breathed as I ran into his arms..."

"We did it!" Smalls said as he hugged me...

"You did it..." Bazil said as he hugged Smalls and I hugged Troy...

"Can we eat now? Please?" Joselyn laughed...

"Yes we can – we're just as hungry as you are..." Bazil laughed as we all went into the kitchen... and I started crying again...

"Damn – stop crying!" Keisha laughed as she started crying too...

"I can't help it... I'm so happy..." I cried as Bazil pulled me close to him...

"Hurry up and make them plates – maybe if we get some food in their mouths they'll concentrate on something else..." Smalls laughed...

"Awww shit!" Keisha and Troy said in unison as we all laughed. We all got plates... started eating... started drinking... and then there was another knock on the door...

"Bazil... somebody's at the door..." Smalls said as he started eating...

"It's for you..." Bazil said as we all continued eating..."

"Yo – aaight – you lucky I love you…" Smalls said as he got up to get the door…"

"Yo Bazil…" Troy laughed… "You funny…"

"It's for him…" Bazil said…

"How you know?" Troy asked…

"'Cause I do…" Bazil answered…

"Fina… Smalls said as he opened the door…

"Hey…" his wife, Josefina, said as she came inside…

"What are you doing here?" Smalls asked…

"Aren't you happy to see me?"

"Always…" Smalls said as he pulled her into a kiss…

"That's more like it…" she said as they continued kissing…

"C'mon… I'll introduce you…" Smalls said as he brought her into the kitchen… "Everyone… this is my love… my wife… Josefina…" Smalls beamed. I started tearing up as I remembered our conversation…

"Dammit Beautiee – why are you crying now?" Keisha laughed…

"I'm crying because I'm happy… dammit!" I laughed. I got up from the table and went over to Smalls and Josefina… "I'm Beautiee…" I said as I hugged her…

"It's nice to meet you…" she said as she hugged me back…

"Nice to see you Josefina…" Bazil said as he smiled and winked at her…

"Nice to see you too Bazil..." she said...

"This is Sam, his wife Joselyn, her mother Sheila, Keisha, and Troy..." I said as I acknowledged everyone at the table...

"Are you hungry?" Smalls asked...

"Yes I am..." she answered...

"Here..." Bazil said as he handed her a plate of everything...

"Something to drink?" Smalls asked...

"Maybe after I eat..." she answered...

"Can we talk?" Smalls asked...

"Sure..." she answered as she smiled. Smalls took her by the arm and they left the kitchen...

"I didn't even know Smalls was married..." Keisha said. "Me either..." Troy said.

"He doesn't really talk about his wife..." Bazil said...

"Why not?" Sheila asked...

"He likes to keep his private life private..." Bazil answered...

"C'mon – let's go dance this food and drink off..." I said. We all got up from the table and went into the living room...

"Where'd they go?" Sheila asked...

"They're in the library..." Bazil answered. Sheila, Joselyn, and Keisha ran to the floor to dance with me when Beyoncé's 'Love On Top' started playing. Bazil, Sam, and Troy laughed and fell on each other at our attempt to sing while doing the dance. It started out okay... but went left quickly...

"Nothing's Perfect!" Keisha laughed as she pushed in front of us, tripped, fell, and caused me to fall on top of her...

"Aaahhhh..... Haaa.... Haaa...." We all laughed...

"Damn girl – how much did you have to drink?" Keisha laughed...

"Not as much as you..." I laughed... "I get better when I'm drunk!" I laughed...

"C'mon ladies!" Bazil and Troy said as they both tried to help us up... and we pulled them down on the floor with us...

"What the hell kinda dancing is that?" Sam laughed...

"Line dancing – they all fell down – in a line!" Sheila laughed...

"Aaahhhh..... Haaa.... Haaa...." We all laughed. We were so busy having fun we didn't see Smalls slip out with Josefina... "Oh shit – let's do this!" I said as I jumped up off the floor to dance to One Wine by Machel Montano & Sean Paul...

"I love the way she looks, pretty face and smile hold down on me..." Bazil and I started dry fucking but Keisha and Troy beat us to it. Sam and Joselyn were dancing like they danced on their wedding day but they were too busy looking at each other to notice anyone else, and Sheila had gone into the kitchen to get us more drinks... "And the way she move, in a di dance whining her body. It didn't take no time, I'm about to fall in love from one whine..." When Sheila came back into the living room with the drinks we were all whining and grinding so she sat down to finish her drink while she watched us...

"Now this is my music!" Sheila said as Where Do U Want Me to Put It started playing...

"Shit – this e'rbody's music!" Troy laughed as we all started dancing... "Time to get off..." Troy sang...

"Let's get it on..." Sam sang...

"Anytime you're in the mood to groove give me a call..." Bazil sang...

"Just say the word..." Troy sang...

"I'll be right there..." Sam sang...

"Baby I'm gonna fill you up with tender love and care..." Bazil sang...

"It's all to make you feel good... To carry you to ecstasy..." Troy sang as he pulled Keisha close to him and held her...

"If you gimmie directions, communicate to me..." Bazil sang as he pulled me close to him...

"Baby, tell me where do you want me to put it..."Sam sang as he pulled Joselyn close to him...

"Right here!" Joselyn and Sheila both said in unison as they both pointed between their legs...

"Aaaaa….. Haaaa….. Haaa…..!" we all laughed as we kept dancing…

"It's time to come closer… 'cause I've got the urge…" Troy sang to Keisha…

"So baby can we do it once or twice just to rehearse…" Sam sang to Joselyn…

"When can we work it out, when can we work it out now…" Sheila sang…

"Or do you like it when I get my groove on round and around and around and around…" Bazil sang to me…

"It's all to make us feel good in love even the blind can see, if we give you directions, just put it over here 'cause we told you where… where we want you to put it!" Keisha, Joselyn, and I sang…

"Put it right here – 'cause I'm tired…" Sheila said as she sat down…"

"Aaaaa….. Haaaa….. Haaa!" we all laughed as we kept dancing…

"Is it right here… is it over there… when we're makin' love…" Troy, Sam and Bazil sang…

"Y'all love to get us off!" Keisha, Joselyn, and I sang. We danced until the song was finished and then Sheila got up to leave…

"It's past my bed time – good night y'all…" she yawned…

"Yea… some of us have to work tomorrow…" Sam laughed…

"True… and my boss has a zero tolerance policy for lateness…" Joselyn laughed…

"I guess you better get going then... wouldn't want you to get in trouble with the boss..." Bazil laughed...

"Take some food – please..." I said.

"Can we take some drink too?" Sam asked...

"Sure..." I said as they went into the kitchen...

"Well... I guess we'll get going too..." Troy said...

"Guess again..." Bazil said...

"Ummmmm... okay... I guess we're staying Keisha..." Troy said as he sat back down...

"We're ready..." Sheila said as they came out of the kitchen...

"Thank you for everything – I love y'all..." I said as we took turns hugging each other...

"We love you too – see you soon..." Sheila said as she left and Joselyn and Sam followed.

"What's up Bazil?" Troy asked...

"You tell me..." Bazil said...

"Tell you what?"

"So... you have nothing you wanna ask me?"

"Oh... Yea..."

"Ask me..."

"Trevor?"

"What about him?"

"C'mon Keisha... let's let the men talk..." I said as I got up and she followed me into the kitchen...

"Let's put the food away and clean this up…" I said as I started to put the food away…

"Beautiee… wait a minute…"

"I'm okay Keisha…" I said as I went to put the baked ziti in the fridge… and dropped it… "Dammit!" I said as I started crying…

"You goin' be alright…" Keisha said as she hugged me…

"I messed up bad…" I cried…

"Wait a minute… how'd you mess up?"

"I slept with Trevor…"

"So did Bazil – it's crazy - but I understand it…"

"You do?"

"I'on know if I could'a done it if Troy cheated on me with a man – but if Troy cheated on me with a woman – I'd definitely cheat on him – that shit hurts – he'd need to know how it feels…"

"I hurt myself more than I hurt Bazil…"

"Really?"

"Yea… I never wanted him…"

"He wanted you though - if he didn't – he would'a told you no…"

"That's exactly what I said!" I laughed as we both cleaned up the baked ziti…

"Can I ask you a personal question?"

"It doesn't get more personal than this…" I laughed…

"Have you always liked women?"

"I never liked women..."

"Okay wait – I'm confused..."

"I always wanted to try a threesome with a woman and my husband – but I don't want to be with women..."

"Ohh... okay... so how did you wind up with Sonia?"

"Well... she was a shoulder to cry on..."

"Okay... I get that... so how'd you end up in bed with her?"

"We went out for drinks... she started telling me how she'd never been with a man because she saw how men treated her mother..."

"So she chose to be with women?"

"That's what she said..." I answered as we continued to put the food away...

"Hmmmmm... I don't get it..."

"I did it... and I don't get it either..."

"Did what?"

"I had sex with her... but I still love me some dick!" I laughed...

"Ohhh!" Keisha laughed...

"She tried to get me to leave Bazil for her..."

"Oh Shit! For real?"

"Yea... she kept telling me she couldn't understand how I could want Bazil after everything he put me through – she asked me if the dick was that good..." I didn't realize Bazil was standing there listening...

"What'd you tell her?"

"I told her – in a word – yes…" I laughed…

"She really wanted you to leave Bazil? For her?"

"Yea…"

"Damn Beautiee – you turned her out!" Keisha laughed…

"I didn't mean too – I never led her on – she knew I loved Bazil…"

"This shit's crazy!"

"It is! I wish I never invited her…" I said as I started to cry…

"C'mere girl – stop crying…"

"You don't understand – if I never invited her – none of this would'a happened!"

"You can't blame yourself Beautiee… you didn't know what would happen…"

"You don't understand…"

"What don't I understand Beautiee?"

"I didn't do any of it – she did!"

"Wait – what?"

"I invited her to come over – she told me the shit wasn't like the movies – she asked me if I was sure – I said yes…"

"Okay – so how is that you're fault – she said yes!"

"Because… she's the one that let Trevor in the house…" I whispered…

"Oooohhh!"

"I didn't realize it until Trevor dropped the gun when she got shot… he grabbed her, held her, and told me she wasn't supposed to die…" I cried…

"So – wait a minute – Sonia and Trevor set y'all up?"

"Yes! And it's all my fault!" I cried…

"Beautiee – it's fucked up – but it's not your fault – if anything – it's Bazil's damn fault!"

"That's what he says…"

"He does?"

"Yea…"

"Well he's right… I'on know if I would'a stayed with Troy after all that…"

"Really?"

"I love Troy to death… but I don't know if I could'a dealt with all that – and you went to jail too – Bazil needs to thank God for you…"

"He does… and I thank God for him too…"

"Really?"

"Yea… Bazil asked me to marry him again… and I said yes…"

"Damn – you really do love him…"

"Yes… I do…"

"He's a lucky man…"

"I'm the lucky one…"

Chapter 14

Bazil closed the door, picked me up and carried me upstairs without saying a word. Once we got upstairs he took me into the bedroom and tossed me on the bed...

"Come here my Thirst Quencher..." I said with open arms and spread legs. Bazil climbed on the bed slowly, crawled between my legs, laid down on top of me, and cried on my shoulder. I didn't say anything – I knew he needed to cry. He'd been strong for weeks – kissing my tears, reassuring me that everything was going to be okay – even when he wasn't sure of it – and now that everyone was gone – now that I was home – he could let it all out. I held him and let him cry as much as he needed to until he looked up at me and spoke...

"You promised me you'd never leave me..." he whispered through tear-soaked eyes...

"I'm sorry..." I whispered as I started to cry. He sat up on the bed and I sat up with him before he continued...

"I love you so much Beautiee... I'd give my life for you..."

"I know..."

"When I asked you to run with me... I needed you to say yes..." he said tearing up again...

"I wanted to Bazil..." I said as I cried...

"Then why didn't you?"

"I didn't want you to lose everything..."

"Beautiee..." he said as he pulled me into a kiss... "You're my everything..."

"Oh Bazil..." I cried...

"When I say I gotchu... please believe... I gotchu..."

"I know... I was scared Bazil..."

"Beautiee – you had nothing to be afraid of – I was ready – Smalls was ready..."

"Smalls?"

"Yes Beautiee..."

"I'm sorry... I didn't mean to hurt you..." I cried...

"I know baby... I know..." he said as he kissed me again...

"I didn't want to be on the run... I wanted to be free..."

"And you would have been..."

"How?"

"You would have been free – free from everything you went through in prison..." he whispered...

"It was so hard..." I whispered as I continued to cry...

"I know baby... I wanted to be there for you... I couldn't be there... I couldn't protect you... you could've died... and you would've gone through all that for nothing!" he said as he started crying again...

"Please don't cry Bazil... I'm sorry..." I cried...

"Beautiee... you have nothing to be sorry for... you were in there because of me...

"No Bazil..."

"Yes Beautiee... I'm the one that was with Trevor... I should've ended it with him as soon as I married you..."

"Bazil... I know you didn't mean to hurt me..."

"No I didn't... and I'll never hurt you again... I promise..." he cried as he kissed me again... "And I promise... they're going to regret the day they crossed me... and they'll regret the day they hurt you... every last one of them..."

"Bazil... please... it's over... I'm home... I missed you so much it hurt... let me make it up to you... please..." I whispered before I pushed him down on the bed, moved down between his legs, took his dick out his pants, and wrapped my mouth around it...

"Mmmmmm.... Yeesss... suck it..." he moaned as I sucked his dick slowly and deliberately. I moved up further on the bed and leveraged myself on his thighs, using my hands along with my mouth so I could take his dick in further... "Beautiee... Fuck..." he moaned as he grabbed my head with both his hands and fucked my mouth. I could feel his thighs tightening and I relaxed my throat so I could take him in a little further... "I'm cummmmmiiinnnggg.... Uggggghhhh!" I swallowed every drop, closed my eyes, and continued sucking softly while Bazil watched... "Mmmmmm... I missed this..." Bazil breathed as he played in my hair. I stopped sucking for a moment...

"I've dreamed of this moment so many times..." I said and then I went back to sucking...

"So have I..." Bazil breathed. I stopped sucking again...

"Did you... play with yourself while I was away?" I asked before I started sucking again...

"Mmmmmm...." He moaned... "No... I wanted to give it to you... Ooohhh.... Beautiee..."

"Mmmmmm... I'm... glad... you... waited... I was... starving..." I said between sucks...

"Come here Beautiee..." Bazil said as he pulled me up to his chest, took my face in his hands, and kissed me hard... "So..." he asked me between kisses... "Did you... play... with... yourself... while... you... were... away..."

"No... I wanted... you..."

"Did... your... pussy... ache..."

"Yeeess...."

"Did... your... pussy... throb..."

"Yyyeeessss...."

"Did... you... imagine... me... fucking... you?" he asked and then he turned me down on my back, opened my pants, and began playing with my pussy...

"Oh Bazil... yeeessss..." Bazil covered my mouth with his and tongued me hard as he pushed two fingers inside me and began finger-fucking me... "Mmmmmm.... MmmmMmmm.... MmmmMmmm..." I moaned in Bazil's mouth. Bazil increased his speed and I started coming all over his hand... "MmmmMmmm! MmmmMmmm! MmmmMmmm! MmmmMmmm!" I moaned in Bazil's mouth as I came. Bazil took his hand out my pants, licked his fingers, and asked... "So... is that what you imagined..."

"Yessss... my Thirst Quencher..." I breathed...

"Let me show you what I imagined..." he said as he lifted me up, pulled off my shirt, removed my bra, laid me back down, and began kissing and sucking my breasts...

"Bazil..." I moaned as I pulled him down between my legs...

"Yes... Beautiee..." he answered as he removed my panties and my pants...

"Fuck me..." I breathed...

"Not yet..." he said as he kissed his way down my body... "I'm not done showing you what I imagined..." he said as he spread my legs and dove in...

"Baaazzziiillll!" I screamed as he began sucking my clit hard while simultaneously finger-fucking me...

"Yes... Beautiee..."

"Huuuu... Huuu... Huuu... Huuu... Huuu..." I moaned as I thrashed my head back and forth. "Mmmmmm... just like I imagined..." Bazil said and then went back to sucking my clit hard again... "Huuuu... Huuu... Huuu... Huuu... Huuu... Bazil...I'm cummmmmmiiiinnnnggg!" I screamed as I arched my back and body up off the bed. Bazil continued to suck on my clit softly and finger-fuck me as my orgasm subsided until I spoke... "Bazil..." I panted...

"Yesss... Beautiee..." he answered while continuing to finger-fuck me...

"I'm a bit sensitive...

"Is that right?"

"Yesss..."

"Hmmmmm... let me see..." he said before starting to suck on my clit again...

"Huuu... Huuu... Bazil..."

"Hmmmmm... you are a bit sensitive... I'll give you a minute before I continue..." he said before getting up on his knees. Once he was up on his knees he removed his shirt, slid his pants and boxers off his ass, kicked them off his body, climbed up on top of me, and started kissing me...

"Mmmmmm..." I moaned... I missed you...

"I missed you too..." We continued kissing and holding each other for a few moments and then Bazil spoke... "Beautiee..."

"Yes... my Thirst Quencher..." I answered between kisses...

"Do... you... remember... what... I... told you?"

"When?"

"When... you... left... me... and... came... back..." he answered as he slid inside me and began fucking me...

"Yeeessss..."

"What... did... I... tell... you?"

"You... said... if... I... ever... left... you... again... oooohhh..."

"Go on..."

"You'd... fuck... me... to... death..."

"What... did... you... do?"

"I... didn't... mean... to... oooohhh..."

"I... know... but... you... did..."

"It... wasn't... my... fault..."

"Doesn't... matter... you... still... left... me... you... know... what... that... means..."

"Ohhhh... Bazil... Fuck me... Yeeesss..."

"So... tell... me... what... does... that... mean?"

"It means... it means... Bazil... don't stop..."

"What... does... it... mean?" he growled as he started pounding my pussy..."

"It... means... I... I... have... to... pay... Aaaaagggghhhh!"

Chapter 15

"I'm ready to go back to work... at your company... and mine..."

"Why do you want to keep your LLC?"

"Because I do..."

"Well – Smalls can help us set it up where your LLC is underneath my corporation – this way we have one company together, protect our assets, streamline the business bookkeeping, and simplify our marketing."

"I like that..."

"You do?"

"Yes..."

"Hmmm... I thought you'd object..."

"Why?"

"Well... I thought you might want to continue to be a Sole Proprietor..."

"I'm going to continue to be a Sole Proprietor... under my husband..." I said as I moved closer to Bazil...

"Mmmmm... under your husband... I like that..." he breathed before pulling me into a kiss...

"So do I..." I breathed as I kissed him back...

"Are you hungry?"

"Always..." I breathed as he laid me down on the bed and climbed on top of me...

"Let me feed you then..." Bazil said before kissing me fully...

"Bazil..."

"Yesss... Beautiee..." he said in between kisses...

"We... need... to... talk..."

"Okay..." he sighed disappointedly... "What's wrong?" he asked as he rolled off of me, lay down beside me, and propped himself up on his elbow...

"Nothing..." I sighed as I turned to face him..."

"Beautiee..." he said as he stroked my hair... "Talk to me..."

"I want to tell my story..."

"Wait a minute..."

"I want to tell my story..."

"You mean... about us?"

"Yes..."

"Hmmmmm... I don't know..."

"My readers already know what happened to me... and so does everybody else..."

"I was hoping we could put it behind us..." Bazil sighed...

"Okay... never mind..." I sighed as I went to get up but Bazil pulled me back down onto the bed...

"Beautiee... wait..."

"Forget it... I won't do it..."

"You can do it..."

"Really?"

"Yes..."

"It's going to be very personal..."

"I know..."

"And you're okay with that?"

"Not really..."

"Then I won't do it..."

"You have to do it..."

"I don't understand... I thought you didn't want me to do it?"

"I don't want you to... but I know you need to..."

"I still don't understand..."

"You've been through a lot... you have a story to tell..."

"Yes I do..."

"And you want to tell your story..."

"Okay..."

"And I'm a big part of your story..."

"Yes you are..."

"Maybe that's a good thing..."

"It is... it is..." I said as I pulled him into a kiss..."

"So... have you started working on your story yet?"

"I started working on my story when I was in jail..."

"You did?"

"Yea..."

"How'd you find the time?"

"Once I started writing, I couldn't stop – I wrote the song, and then I started writing my story..."

"Where'd you get the pen and paper?"

"Deputy Warden Hein gave it to me... he said it would keep me outta trouble while I was in there..."

"Hmmmmm... that was nice of him... I'll have to thank him..."

"I already tried to thank him – and he refused..."

"He refused?"

"Yea – after he gave me the pad he let me talk to you..."

"Yes... I remember..."

"So I tried to give him a hug and he refused..."

"Yea – Nathan's like that – keeps him from being brought up on charges of sexual harassment..."

"Oh right – I didn't think of that..."

"So can I read what you've written so far?"

"You promise not to critique it?"

"What'da you mean?"

"I mean don't be my publisher – don't be my editor – don't correct my grammar – don't change my words – don't make suggestions – just read it!" I snapped...

"Okay Beautiee..." he laughed... "I promise..."

"Okay... here..." I said as I pulled my pad out, handed it to Bazil, and he started reading:

Chapter One

I was completely done. I was psychologically, emotionally, and physically drained. I knew I shouldn't be turning to alcohol, but it was either a drink or a shotgun and since I couldn't get my hands on a shotgun, a drink would have to do. I sat there admiring the glass of amaretto sour in front of me, picked up the cherry, and slid it into my mouth. I closed my eyes, tilted my head back slightly, and imagined the liquor going down my throat, quenching my thirst, and numbing the pain I was in. I opened my eyes and as I reached for the glass, he wrapped his hand around my hand and held the drink with me. "Who are you?" I asked as I watched him pick up the glass and take a sip with both our hands holding it...

"I'm your Thirst Quencher," he answered as we put the glass down, he leaned towards me, and began kissing me slowly and softly, sliding his tongue in my mouth, allowing me to suck the amaretto flavor. I couldn't take my eyes off of him. It was hot inside and out, and I admired the

sweat dripping from his chocolate temples. We picked up the glass again and he took another sip, but this time when he leaned in to kiss me he used his tongue to pour the amaretto into my mouth, sliding his tongue in a little deeper, allowing me to suck and swallow. We lifted the glass again and before he could take a sip, I brought the glass to my mouth and gulped the rest of the drink down. He looked at me with such a sad face and turned to leave but before he could, I turned him back towards me, took his face in my hands, and kissed him fully in the mouth, sliding my tongue into his so he could suck the amaretto flavor. We pulled away from kissing and I was relieved to see I changed his mind.

"Who are you?" he asked.

"I'm Beautiee," I answered as I lowered my head.

"Look at me," he whispered as he gently placed his hand under my chin and picked my head up. "What happened?"

"Long story," I answered as I tried to lower my head but couldn't. When I tried to turn my head away from him, he wouldn't allow it.

"Look at me," he whispered as he turned my head to face him. "I've got all night," he said as he looked into my face.

"I don't want to…"

"It's okay… you don't have to," he said as he stood up. "Come with me… please…" he

159

whispered as he held out his hand. I stood up, took his hand, and allowed him to lead me to the elevator. I knew where we were going but I didn't care... I needed to numb the pain I was in and I was going to numb it one way or the other. The way I figured, this way was better than a shotgun. When the elevator doors opened, I realized where I was and started having second thoughts...

"I can't do this," I whispered as I backed up into the elevator. He stood in the door, blocking it from closing...

"Don't leave me Beautiee... please..." he whispered as he extended his hand for me to take. I took his hand again and allowed him to lead me out the elevator down the hall and into his room. Once inside, I looked around the suite, admiring the décor. The master bath was off to the right with two sinks, porcelain countertops, recessed lighting, and marble floors, and a shower build for two. The king size bed was to the left, made up with brown, cream, and red comforters and pillows. In the middle of the room was a chocolate chaise lounge, and to the right of that was a desk with a computer, a lamp, paper, pens, and a phone. "Make yourself comfortable," he said as he sat down on his bed and patted, motioning for me to sit down next to him.

"I'd like to take a shower," I said as I opened the closet door and took the robe off the hanger.

"Whatever you want," he said, looking at me seductively.

"I need another drink" I said as I walked over to the chaise lounge and sat down.

"Amaretto sour?" he asked.

"I need something a little stronger... something to take the edge off..."

"I'll make you another amaretto," he said, completely ignoring my request. When he sat down on the chaise lounge next to me with the drink, I reached for the drink but he playfully pulled it away, smiling. "Say please," he commanded.

"Please," I said sarcastically.

"You can do better than that," he replied just as sarcastically.

"Look," I said as I turned to face him.

"Yes Beautiee?" he said as he turned to look at me. I could tell he was really enjoying this...

"Who are you?" I asked.

"I'm your Thirst Quencher," he answered, still holding the drink...

"The ice is beginning to melt... and I'm really thirsty..."

"Here," he said as he handed me the glass and I wrapped my hand around his hand.

"Thank you," I replied, slowly taking a sip and pulling the glass away. He watched me swallow and as we both dropped the glass, he pushed me back onto the chaise lounge and began *kissing me forcefully. He slowed down when he sensed I wasn't enjoying it and continued kissing me softly and sensually, sucking my tongue, tasting the amaretto. "MmmmMmmm..." he moaned between kisses, moving from my mouth to my neck...*

"Don't..." I whispered...

"Please..." he panted while continuing to kiss my neck...

"I... need..." I tried to explain between kisses...

"You... need... to... let... me... be... your... Thirst... Quencher...

"Shower..." I panted...

"Okay... I'll join you..." I didn't want him to...

"No..." I panted...

"Please..."

"I'll be right back..."

"I'm... coming... with... you..."

"Okay..." I relented.

"Come with me," he said as he stood up and reached for my hand. I took his hand, stood up, picked up the robe, and let him lead me to the shower. I stepped into the bathroom and watched him come up behind me in the mirror. He unzipped my dress and began kissing my neck as he slid my dress off my shoulders and it fell to the floor. He was pleasantly surprised when he saw I was naked underneath. He quickly disrobed, dropping his clothes to the floor,

turning me around to face him. His look quickly changed from seductive to hurt when he saw the bruises on my body. I tried to look away but he placed his hand under my chin, turned me to him, pulled me close to him, and kissed me. He reached to turn on the shower, took me by the hand, and let me inside. I stood underneath the water and let it soothe me as he reached for the shampoo, squirting some in his hands. He began to massage my scalp while simultaneously kissing the back of my neck.

"Mmmmmm..... that's nice..." I moaned as I began to relax...

"Ouch... what the... oh my God... Beautiee..." he whispered as he pulled his left hand away to look at the blood. I couldn't turn to look at him. I just continued to stand under the water, facing the wall, until he turned me around to face him... "Beautiee... this is glass... I need to check to see if you're still bleeding... you might need stitches... let me rinse this out... I'll try not to hurt you... be still..." he said as the shampoo ran down my head and face... "Turn your head this way... it looks like you might need stitches...

"No... I said, shaking my head.

"Let's get you cleaned up," he said completely ignoring me, until... "What are you doing?"

"What does it feel like I'm doing?" I asked him as I continued 'washing' his dick.

"It... feels... nice..." he moaned as I continued soaping him up and down. I loved watching the creamy lather run down his chocolate body.

"Ouch," I said as he started soaping my bruises.

"I'm sorry Beautiee," he whispered as he pulled me into a passionate kiss. I could feel his erection against me and I wanted him – needed him. I felt safe and secure in his arms and I wanted to stay in them for as long as I could. We stopped kissing and I wrapped my arms around him as he continued to hold me against him. "Come here," he whispered as he led me out the shower towards the bench. I sat down and he gently towel-dried my hair, being particularly careful on the left side of my head. "It looks like the bleeding stopped... you may not need stitches," he said as he continued to dry me off and then himself. When he was finished he lifted me up off the bench, careful not to grab me by my bruises, carried me to the bed, and gently laid me down on the bed. He lay behind me and pulled me close to him, spooning me, kissing me softly on my neck and shoulder.

"You... feel... so... good...," I yawned as I drifted off the sleep...

Bazil didn't say anything. He put the pad down on the night stand and looked at me with tears in his eyes. He pulled me close to him, kissed me, and held me as he cried for a few moments and then he spoke... "Oh my God... Beautiee... I love you so much..."

"I love you too... my Thirst Quencher..."

"I know... I can't believe it... the way you wrote about me... you made me seem so gentle... so loving..."

"You are gentle... you are loving..."

"I saw you... and I knew..."

"I knew too..."

"Were you really thinking about killing yourself?"

"I was in pain... and I was on a mission to numb it as best I could... and the bar was right there..."

"And so was I..."

"And you're still here..."

"Damn right I am..." he said as he pulled me into a kiss...

"So you like my story so far?"

"I love it..."

"It's going to get worse..."

"I know..."

"You're still okay with it?"

"Yesss..."

"Good..."

"So... are you going to leave anything out of your story?" Bazil asked as he started kissing me on my neck..."

"I'm an erotic fiction publisher..." I moaned... "My readers expect erotica..."

"Mmmmmm…." He moaned as he kissed me… I can't wait to read it…"

"I can't wait to write it…" I moaned as he lay me down on the bed…"

"Will I get to read more?" he asked as he climbed on top of me, spread my legs, slid himself inside me, and started thrusting…

"Yeesss…" I moaned.

Chapter 16

"What time is it?" I yawned...

"It's a little after 12..." Bazil answered as he bent down to kiss me...

"Mmmm... why didn't you wake me up?"

"It's been so long since I've seen you sleeping peacefully..."

"I missed this bed..." I sighed...

"Is that all you missed?" he asked, looking at me mischievously...

"I missed you..."

"Oh yea?"

"Bazil!"

"I missed you too..." he said as he bent down to kiss me again...

"I missed waking up, having morning sex, and going to work with you..." I said as I sat up...

"I missed that too..." he said as he took off his robe, pulled back the covers, and got back in bed with me...

"Did you work while I was away?"

"I tried... but I couldn't..."

"That was the worst thing I've ever been through in my life..."

"I know... I'm sorry..."

"Let's get married…"

"Okay…"

"Let's renew our vows in the courthouse…"

"Okay…"

"Ooohhh… I have an idea…"

"What?"

"Let's ask Judge Duffey to marry us again… in his old chambers!" I laughed…

"I love it!"

"You do?"

"Beautiee…" he breathed as he kissed me… "I… love… anything… that… makes… you… happy…"

We called Smalls and asked him to contacted Judge Duffey. After Smalls contacted him, we received the following letter:

Dear Mr. & Mrs. Osgood,

I have to admit it – when I heard from your attorney, I was nervous to say the least; however, once your attorney explained why he was calling, I was pleasantly surprised.

I also have to admit – you are the only couple that has been in my court room for a criminal proceeding and then turn around and ask me to officiate the renewal of your vows, as well as your friends. The fact that you would choose me is, in itself, an honor and a privilege, and I am truly humbled.

I am happy to do this for you. My wife is more excited than I am – especially because she's one of your biggest fans.

I look forward to seeing you and your friends on the beach on Valentine's Day at 5pm.

Cordially,

Judge Duffey

"I'm so happy..."
"So am I..."
"I can't wait until Valentine's Day..."
"Neither can I..."
"Let's go upstairs..."
"Okay" he said as he took my hand and led me upstairs to the bedroom...

Chapter 17

"Come with me..." Bazil said as he took me by the hand and led me to the library. I started to turn around and go towards the living room but I changed my mind and became curious as Bazil opened the door...

"Ooohhh... Bazil... It's beautiful!" I sighed as I went in to look around...

"You really like it?"

"I love it!" I exclaimed as I threw my arms around his neck and kissed him hard...

"Mmmm... I'm glad you're happy..." he breathed as he held me. The room was painted a light, airy cream. The sofa I caught him on was gone and was replaced by two Allegro L-Desks – one on the left side and one on the right – and both desks were positioned so we could see out the bay window. Behind his desk on the left was a brown Erwin Executive Swivel Tilt Chair, and behind my desk on the right was beige Katherine Home Office Chair. There was on Alegro Computer Credenza & Hutch on my desk and there was a Brookhaven 3-piece Bookcase on the wall in front of his desk. A Dutchess Chair was in the corner near the door and on the wall in front of my desk was a paisley sand Dutchess Sofa with cream and fudge-stripped pillows. A Black Juliet Area Rug tied everything together...

"I love my chair!" I exclaimed as I sat behind my desk...

"You look good..."

"Sit in your chair – I wanna see!"

"Okay..." he said as he sat in his chair...

"I love the view..."

"I love you..."

"I love you too...

"Go sit in the chair by the door..."

"Okay!" I squealed as I go up, hurried over to the chair, posed, and took a selfie...

"Get up..." I stood up, Bazil came behind me, sat in the chair, pulled me down onto his lap, and took a selfie... "Now that's a picture..." he said as he looked at it and then he showed it to me...

"I love it...

"I love you..." he said as he pulled my face to his, put his tongue in my mouth, and tongued me down. I tried to pull away from him but he held me by the back of my head...

"Beautiee... stop trying to pull away from me..."

"I wanna go sit on the couch..."

"Okay..." he said as he let go of me. I got up off his lap, went over to the couch, stretched out, and held my arms open...

"Come here my Thirst Quencher..." Bazil got up, came over to the couch, lay on top of me, and I wrapped my arms around him as we started kissing...

"I love you so much..." Bazil breathed in my ear...

"I love you too..."

"Let me make love to you..." he breathed as he kissed me again...

"Here?" in the library?"

"Yeesss..."

"I don't want to mess up the sofa..."

"You won't..."

"Yes... I will..."

"I don't care..." he breathed as he opened my pants and pushed them down off my waist, past my knees, and down to my ankles. I kicked them off my ankles and opened my legs and Bazil got up on his knees, opened his pants, took his dick out, and began stroking it... "You want this?"

"Yes..." I breathed. Bazil lay down on top of me, eased himself inside me, and kissed me as he began thrusting...

"Hmmph... Hmmph... Hmmph... Hmmph..."

"Mmmph... Mmmph... Mmmph... Mmmph..." I put one leg up on the back of the sofa, dropped my other leg down off the couch, grabbed his ass, and pushed him in deeper...

"Hmmph... Hmmph... Hmmph... Hmmph..."

"Mmmph... Mmmph... Mmmph... Mmmph..." Bazil put his arms underneath my back, held me tighter, and started thrusting harder...

"HMMPH! HMMPH! HMMPH! HMMPH!"

"MMMPH! MMMPH! MMMPH! MMMPH!" Bazil was thrusting harder, deeper, and faster and he was coming with me...

"HMMPH! HMMPH! HMMPH! HMMPH!"

"MMMPH! MMMPH! MMMPH! MMMPH!" Bazil slowed down but didn't stop as our orgasms subsided and we continued kissing...

"Mmmm.... You needed that..." I breathed...

"So did you..." he breathed...

"I can't wait 'till Valentine's Day..."

"Neither can I..."

"I'm hungry..."

"You want more..."

"Always..."

"Let's go get something to eat..."

"Okay..."

"Then we'll go upstairs..."

"Okay..."

"Then I'll give you more..."

"Okay..." Bazil got up, extended his hand, took mine, helped me up off the couch, pulled me to him, and held me... "Thank you..." I breathed...

"You're welcome..." he said as we walked out the library and into the kitchen... "What would you like?"

"You know what – I'm in the mood for pizza!" I laughed...

"We don't have any pizza in the fridge..." Bazil laughed...

"I know – let's order a large pie – with meat!"

"Ummm... what kind of meat would you like?" he asked as he smiled at me mischievously...

"I want sausage, pepperoni, meatball, and bacon – oh – and I want some potato chips..."

"Beautiee..."

"Yeesss...."

"Beautiee..."

"Yeesss..."

"Beautiee!" Bazil exclaimed as he grabbed me by the shoulders...

"Yes Bazil?"

"Where were you?" he laughed...

"I was... dreaming..." I sighed...

"Musta been a hell of a dream..." Bazil laughed...

"You didn't even hear me calling you..."

"It was..." I sighed...

"You wanna eat here or you wanna eat upstairs?"

"Hmmm... upstairs..." I sighed...

"Okay – we'll stay downstairs until the pizza comes... and then we'll go upstairs..."

"Okay..." I sighed as I looked out the window...

Chapter 18

"Cheryl?"

"Yes Mrs. Osgood?"

"Staff meeting in one hour..." I said as I left before she could ask me any questions...

"Oh my God – what happened?" another employee asked...

"We're about to find out..." Cheryl sighed...

"Are you ready for this?" Bazil asked...

"Yea..." I sighed...

"I wish it was happening tomorrow..."

"So do I..." I breathed as we sat down on the sofa and started kissing...

"Where would you like to go on our honeymoon?"

"Somewhere warm... and tropical..."

"Jamaica..."

"That sounds nice..."

"Trinidad..."

"That sounds nice too..."

"Paradise Island..."

"Ooohhh..."

"You like that?"

"Yeesss..."

"Paradise Island…" Bazil said as he pulled me down on top of him and held me…

"I have so much to do…" I sighed…

"All you need to do is show up and say I do…"

"I can't wait to write about this…"

"When you write… do you write about the sex?"

"Oh yea…"

"Do you feel it all over again?"

"Mmmm Hmmm…"

"Do you get wet?"

"Yes…"

"I was just thinking…"

"Uh huh…"

"You write Erotic Fiction…"

"Uh huh…"

"This is actually going to be an autobiography…"

"Uh huh…"

"Are you going to tell them everything?"

"They'll know you got good dick!" I laughed…

"I don't care about that…" he breathed as he started kissing me on my neck…

"Ooohhh… Stop…"

"Is that what you really want?"

"No…"

"That's what I thought…" he said as he ran his hands from my shoulders to the small of my back and kissed me…

"Bazil…"

"Ssshhh…" he whispered as he kissed me, moving his hands from the small of my back to my ass…

"Mrs. Osgood?"

"Yes Joselyn?"

"We're ready…"

"Thank you Joselyn…" I said as I went to get up and Bazil pulled me back down…

"Bazil…"

"Ssshhh…" he said before he kissed me hard…

"Bazil… they're waiting…"

"So am I…" he breathed…

"Let's do this…" I said as I got up and adjusted myself…

"Okay…" Bazil said as he got up, adjusted himself, took my hand, and we walked to the conference room. Everyone got really quiet as we walked in. We went to the head of the table and Bazil put his arm around me before he spoke… "Thank you all for coming. We called this meeting to make an announcement. Osgood Publishing will be closed for Valentine's Day this year…"

"Woo Hoo!"

"Thank you!"

"Yeeaaa!" Bazil and I waited for everyone to quiet down before he continued…

"My wife and I will be renewing our vows on Valentine's Day at 5pm on the Beach here in Milford..."

"Aww..." everyone said in unison...

"If you wish to attend, please confirm your attendance with Joselyn so we know how many seats we need..."

"I'm going!"

"Me too!"

"You know I'm going!"

"We don't have much time – we have a lot to do – so unless anyone has any questions...

"I have a question..." Shadajah said...

"Yes Shadajah?"

"Can we take pictures?"

"Yes – but there's a catch..."

"What's the catch?"

"We get a copy of all of them..."

"I have a question..." A'Licia said...

"Yes A'Licia?"

"Can we bring anybody?"

"We prefer employees and their significant other's only..."

"Oh good – that means I can bring my husband..."

"Yes – you can bring your husband..."

"If there aren't any other questions – we need to get back to the office..." I said. The room was quiet for a few moments... "Okay – see you all soon..." I said as Bazil took my hand, we left the conference room, and we went to Sheila's office...

"Yes?" Sheila said as we walked in...

"Sheila, did you get a chance to speak with your husband?" I asked...

"I did..."

"Will you be joining us?"

"We will..."

"Oh good!" I sighed...

"C'mon Mrs. Osgood – we have work to do..." Bazil said as he smiled at me mischievously..."

"Yes Mr. Osgood..." I sighed as we went to Joselyn's office...

"I'm already on it..." Joselyn laughed...

"You are?" Bazil asked...

'We got this..." Shadajah said...

"Le'me see..." I said as I sat down next to Joselyn...

"Mr. Osgood – pull up a chair..." Joselyn laughed. Bazil pulled up a chair and sat down next to me as we looked on the computer. We looked around and we thought this was the best one..." Joselyn said...

"Hmmm... Gulf Beach Weddings..." Bazil said...

"We thought this was good because you're renewing your vows – the other places want to give you a wedding and a reception..." Shadajah said...

"They have packages that are really nice – from small to large – we were thinking since you invited the employees you might want the Wedding Dreams package – all the packages include a photographer and music – but you can upgrade to a Gazebo and you get up to 30 chairs..." Joselyn said as she showed us the package...

"Ooohhh... this is Beautiful..." I said...

"It's nice..." Bazil agreed...

"They also gave you vows – I think that's nice because we can all say something different..." Joselyn said...

"I like that..." I said...

"The Perfect Package comes with the Gazebo, a photographer, music, and chairs for up to 50 guests..." Shadajah said as she showed us the package...

"Ooohhh... I like this one too!" I exclaimed...

"So do I..." Bazil said...

'This package also gives you an option to add Rose Petals..." Shadajah said...

"Aww..." I said...

"The Celebration Package includes a photographer, 1 hour video service on DVD, 1 hour life music, a Rose Petal Aisle Way, and chairs for up to 100 guests... and you also get the Arch or the Gazebo..." Joselyn said as she showed us the package...

"I want this one!" I squealed...

"Me too..." Bazil said...

"Me too!" Joselyn and Shadajah said in unison and then we all bust out laughing...

"What vows do you want?" Joselyn asked...

"Well – since we're renewing our vows – I like the Commitment Vows..."

"Okay – they have a wedding officiant for the ceremony, and..."

"Joselyn?" I interrupted...

"Yes Mrs. Osgood?"

"Judge Duffey is going to perform the renewal of our vows and his wife is going to witness..."

"Oh... okay..."

"We'll be leaving for the day..." Bazil said as he took my hand and we left the building.

"Let's go to Bridge House..." I said after we got in the car...

"As you wish..." Bazil said as he picked up my hand, kissed it, and drove out the parking lot...

"Welcome to Bridge House Mr. Osgood, Mrs. Osgood – how are you?" the waitress asked...

"We're good – thank you for asking..." Bazil said...

"What can I get you to drink?"

"I'll have a glass of merlot..." I said...

"I'll have one too..." Bazil said...

"I'll be right back with your drinks..." the waitress said as she went to get our drinks...

"I love you…"

"I love you too…"

"Here's your drinks…" the waitress said as she put our glasses of wine on the table… "Are you ready to order?"

"I'll have the BH Burger…" Bazil said…

"Me too…" I said…

"Well done?"

"Well done…" we both answered in unison…

"Okay – I'll be back…" she said as she walked away…

"Here's your burgers…" the waitress said as she put our plates on the table…

"This looks really good…" I said as I picked up the burger and took a bite…"

"Would you like another glass of wine?" the waitress asked…

"Yes please…" I answered…

"And you?" she asked Bazil…

"Mmmm Hmmm…" He acknowledged as he took a bite of his burger. The waitress went to get our wine and we finished eating our burgers and fries…

"Would you like to see a dessert menu?" the waitress asked as she put our glasses of wine on the table…

"I'd love too – I don't have room for dessert – but I'd love to see it…" I laughed…

"I'll bring you the dessert menu… and I'll bring you the check…" she laughed as she went to get both…

"I wish tomorrow was Valentine's Day…" I sighed…

"It is…" Bazil breathed as he kissed me…

"Here's the dessert menu, and here's your check…" the waitress said as she placed them on the table…

"Thank you…" Bazil said…

"You're welcome – always nice to see you…" she said as we got up, paid the check, and left.

Valentine's Day, February 14th, 2020

"Fuck me..." I moaned louder than I usually do...

"Beautiee..." Bazil moaned...

"Bazil... I'm Cummmmiiiinnnngggg! Aaaahhhh!" I screamed...

""Beautiee... Fuck... UUUUGGGGHHHH!" Bazil growled so loud it startled me...

"Wow..." I breathed as I continued riding his dick...

"Yeeessss..."

"I don't know what's gotten into me..." I breathed as he held me by my waist and continued thrusting inside me...

"Meee..." Bazil breathed...

"Yesss..." I breathed as I lay down on him and we started kissing...

"We're getting married... again..."

"Mmmm hmmm..."

"We need to get ready..."

"Mmmm hmmm" Bazil turned me over on my back and now he was on top of me...

"I know you want more..." he breathed as he kissed me...

"Mmmm hmmm…"

"But if I don't get up now… I might not get up at all…"

"Okay…" I sighed and then I pulled him into another kiss…

"Beautiee…"

"I know, I know…"

"Let's go downstairs…" he said as he got up, put on his robe, and held one open for me. I got up put my arms into the sleeves, and Bazil wrapped the robe around me, pulled me to him, and held me…

"I love you so much…" I whispered as I started crying…

"Uh uh…" Bazil said as he kissed my tears…"

"I'm just happy…"

"That's better…" he said as he kissed me again and then we went downstairs to the kitchen… "I'll make coffee…"

"Okay…"

"You still want to go with the Commitment Vows?"

"Yes…"

"Okay…"

"I was just thinking…"

"About what?"

"About how good you looked on our wedding day…"

"Oh yea?"

"When I saw you, I wanted to run to you, rip your clothes off, and fuck you right there..."

"That would've been an interesting video..." Bazil laughed...

When we got to the beach we were in awe. The sun was going down and the orange and blue sunset was the perfect back drop for the ceremony. The waves were cascading slowly up to the sand and I could see the photographer and videographer taking pictures and videos. Unbeknownst to us, we were the last to arrive. There were 25 seats to the left filled with employees their significant others, and a few people we didn't know who took advantage of the opportunity to witness our ceremony. There were also 25 chairs to the right, and the last 15 chairs were filled with more employees. The chairs were white with red ribbons tied to each back leg, and the rose petals were scattered up the walkway to the Gazebo which was also lined with roses. All our friends were on the walkway with the men on the left and the women on the right. Everyone applauded, whistled, and cheered when we started to walk up the walkway and we both started crying. We both took turns hugging Henley, Sheila, Sam, Joselyn, Smalls, Josefina, Troy, and Keisha so it took a bit longer to make it up the walkway to the front of the line but when we finally got there, Judge Duffey handed us tissues, and his wife held a basket with used tissues inside…

"Please put your tissues in here after you finish using them…" she said. Bazil and I did as she asked and then she spoke again… "This basket holds tears of joy from everyone here…"

"Bazil…" I whispered as we started crying again and he pulled me into a kiss…

"My name is Harland Duffey, and this is my wife, Helen. It's been a while since my wife and I have been able to officiate a wedding – especially on Valentine's Day. Each time we do this, we marry the couples that come before us, and we marry each other. We're going to do that again this evening, times five." Judge Duffey waited for everyone to stop applauding, whistling, and cheering before he continued. He came from behind the podium with five bottles of blue sand and his wife came from behind the podium with five bottles of pink sand. Judge Duffey gave each groom a bottle and his wife gave each bride a bottle, and then he went and stood back behind the podium… "I want each couple to come to the Unity Table as I call your name – Bazil & Beautiee…" We went to the Unity Table and his wife put an empty vase on the table…

"You have committed here today to share the rest of your lives with each other. Today, this relationship is symbolized through the pouring of these two individual containers of sand - one representing you Bazil and all that you were, all that you are, and all that you will ever be - the other representing you Beautiee, and all that you were, all that you are, and all that you will ever be. Please pour your sand into the vase…" Bazil and I started pouring our sand into the vase and he continued…

"As these two containers of sand are poured into the third container, the individual containers of sand will no longer exist, but will be joined together as one. Just as these sands can no longer be separated and poured into the individual containers, so will your marriage be." Bazil picked up our vase and we went to the back of the walkway as Troy &Keisha went up to the table, and the Unity of the Sand was repeated with them, Smalls & Josefina, Sam & Joselyn, and finally Henley & Sheila…

"Good evening everyone. Welcome to the celebration of union between Bazil & Beautiee, Troy & Keisha, Jackie & Josefina, Samuel & Joselyn, and Henley & Sheila. Tonight, in front of friends, family, employees, and clients, they honor their commitment to not just gazing at one another, but looking outward together in the same direction. Today, Bazil & Beautiee, Troy & Keisha, Jackie & Josefina, Samuel & Joselyn, and Henley & Sheila, proclaim their love to the world, and we rejoice with and for them. Bazil &

Beautiee, Troy & Keisha, Jackie & Josefina, Samuel & Joselyn, and Henley & Sheila, in presenting yourselves here today you perform a remarkable act of faith. This faith can grow, mature, and endure, but only if you are all determined to make it so. A lasting and growing love is never automatic, nor guaranteed by any ceremony. Let the foundation of your union be the pure love you have for each other, not just at this moment, but for all the days ahead, honor faithfully the statements and commitments that you bring here today. Faults will appear where now you find contentment, and wonder can be crushed by the routine of daily living - but today you resolve that your love will never be blotted out by the commonplace, obscured by the ordinary, or compromised by life's difficulties. Stand fast in that hope and confidence, and believe in your shared future just as strongly as you believe in yourselves and in each other today. Only in this spirit can you create a partnership that will sustain all the days of your lives. Bazil & Beautiee, Troy & Keisha, Jackie & Josefina, Samuel & Joselyn, and Henley & Sheila, we are here to celebrate as you renew this journey together. It is in this spirit that you have come here to today to renew these vows.

"Bazil, Troy, Jackie, Samuel, and Henley, repeat after me to your wives: I take you to be my partner for life. I promise above all else to live in truth with you and to communicate fully and fearlessly, I give you my hand and my heart as a sanctuary of warmth and peace, and pledge my love, devotion, faith and honor as I join my life to yours."

"Beautiee, Keisha, Josefina, Joselyn, and Sheila repeat after me to your husbands: I take you to be my partner for life. I promise above all else to live in truth with you and to communicate fully and fearlessly. I give you my hand and my heart as a sanctuary of warmth and peace, and pledge my love, devotion, faith and honor as I join my life to yours".

"Bazil & Beautiee, Troy & Keisha, Jackie & Josefina, Samuel & Joselyn, and Henley & Sheila, in so much as you all have agreed to live together in Matrimony, have promised your love for each other by renewing your vows, the joining of your hands, I now declare you all to continue to be husbands and wives."

"By the authority vested in me under the laws of the State of Connecticut, I now pronounce you partners for life. Congratulations - you may kiss."

"I love you Mr. Osgood..."
"I love you Mrs. Osgood..."
"We's married..." Keisha said...

"I know that's right..." Troy said...

"Mi esposo mi amor ... My husband, my love..." Josefina said...

"Mi esposa ... mi para siempre ... My wife, my forever..." Smalls said..."

"I love you Joselyn..."

"I love you too Sam..."

"I still love you Sheila..." Henley laughed...

"I still love you too..." Sheila laughed...

"I present to you Mr. and Mrs. Osgood, Mr. & Mrs. Smalls, Mr. & Mrs. Cochran, Mr.& Mrs. Logan, and Mr. & Mrs. Henley!" Judge Duffey shouted. We kissing each other and when So Nice To Be With You started playing we all danced, laughed, hugged, and kissed as each song blended into the next and we didn't realize our time was up until we noticed the staff putting the chairs into the company van...

"Mr. Osgood?" Judge Duffey interrupted as he tapped Bazil on the shoulder...

"Yes your honor..." Bazil answered without looking at him as he held me closer and we continued dancing...

"It's 6:45..."

"Thank you..." Bazil breathed as he pulled me into a deep, passionate kiss... "We better go..." Bazil breathed...

"Okay..." I sighed as we walked along the beach towards the restaurant. When we got up to the entrance, everyone started applauding, whistling, and clapping and we started kissing...

"Congratulations Mr. & Mrs. Osgood – right this way..." the hostess said as we followed her to our table...

"'Bout time y'all got here!" Keisha said as everyone laughed...

"It certainly is..." Bazil said as we sat down on the left side of the table and Judge Duffey and his wife sat down on the right side of the table...

"Good evening..." the waitress greeted... "Congratulations on your vow renewals..."

"Thank you..." we all said in unison...

"May I start you all off with our featured drink, Lousi M. Mautini Caberenet Sauvignon, or would you like something else?"

"We'll have two bottles of Dom Perignon..." Bazil answered...

"Yes Sir – I'll be right back..." she said as she went to get the Champagne...

"Helen, it's so lovely to meet you..." I said...

"Thank you Beautiee – it's lovely meeting you too – it's lovely meeting all of you..." she gushed...

"It's lovely meeting you..." Keisha said...

"Very nice to meet you..." Joselyn said...

"Thank you for witnessing..." Sheila said...

"You're welcome..." Helen said...

"Helen ... eres muy hermosa ... y muy dulce ...   Helen... you are very beautiful... and very sweet..." Josefina said...

"Como eres Helen ... como eres ...   As are you Josefina... as are you..." Helen said. The waitress came over with a waiter and they placed glasses on the table and poured our champagne as we continued...

"It's really nice to meet you Helen – we hardly ever meet the wife of a Judge..." Henley said...

"That's true – we don't ever meet the wives – this is special..." Sam said...

"Your husband is a lucky man..." Smalls said...

"You remind me of my wife..." Troy said as he smiled at Keisha...

"Helen – thank you for coming, witnessing, and celebrating with us..." Bazil said...

"You're welcome – I couldn't imagine a better Valentine's Day..." Helen said...

"Everyone please raise you glass..." Bazil said as he stood up and went to the front of the table... "Beautiee, please stand beside me..." I stood up beside Bazil and then he continued... "Here's to all of us..."

"To all of us..." we all said in unison as we sipped our champagne...

"When we said we wanted to renew our vows on Valentine's Day, you all could have told us you had other plans, but you didn't – instead,

you chose to be here with us and show us love –
and we'll never forget that…"

"Aww…" everyone said in unison…

"Your Honor, Mrs. Duffey – rather than
spend Valentine's Day alone, you chose to be here
with all of us…" Bazil said as he started to fight
back tears… "My wife was right about you – she
said she wanted you to officiate our ceremony
because you gave us our lives back… and…" Bazil
couldn't finish – he started crying, I started
crying, Judge Duffey was tearing up, and his wife
was crying along with everyone else. Judge
Duffey stood up from the table…

"You're welcome…" he said as he hugged
Bazil and then I pulled Bazil into a kiss before we
sat back down…

"Okay – I'ma need y'all to stop… I can't
take it!" Joselyn said as everyone laughed and
wiped their eyes…

"Uh uh – tissues in the basket!" Helen
exclaimed as she put the basket on the table.
Everyone passed their tissues up to the front of
the table and Helen put the tissues in the
basket…

"Y'all 'bout to run outta room – either we
need another basket – or you women need to stop
cryin'!" Henley said as he dabbed his eyes…

"Oh – look who's dabbing his eyes though!"
Sheila said as we all laughed…

"How's everything here?" the waitress
asked as she came back to the table…

"We'll have four plates of each – Fried Calamari, Crab Cakes, Hot Shot Buffalo Wings, Fried Brussel Sprouts, and Mussels Scampi…" Bazil said…

"Four plates of each – got it!" she said as she went to get our appetizers…

"Oh my goodness – Honey look – they have Seafood Pot Pie!" Helen exclaimed…

"You're kidding!" Judge Duffey said…

"Yes Honey – look!" she said as she showed him the menu…

"We're having the Seafood Pot Pie…" Judge Duffey said…

"I'ma get the Seafood Paella…" Troy said…

"I'ma have the Mango Salmon – that shit sounds good!" Keisha exclaimed…

"I'ma have the Seafood Risotto…" Smalls said

"I'll have the Cajun Grilled Atlantic Cod…" Josefina said…

"I'm getting the Blackened Swordfish Gorgonzola…" Joselyn said…

"I'ma have the Grilled Center Cut Filet Mignon…" Sam said…

"I'ma have the Prime Steak Frites…" Henley said…

"I'll have the Chicken Francaise…" Sheila said…

"I'll have the Chicken Francaise too…" I said…

"I'm going to have the Grilled Center Cut Filet Mignon..." Bazil said as the waitress came back over to the table...

"Looks like you've decided..." the waitress said...

"We have..." Bazil said...

"Okay – I'm ready..."

"Two Grilled Center Cut Filet Mignon, Two Chicken Francaise, Two Seafood Pot Pies, and one of every other entrée on the menu..." Bazil said...

"And two more bottles of champagne..." Judge Duffey said...

"Honey..." Helen started to say...

"Helen – I don't have to work tomorrow – I mean not in the court room – I always have to work in the bedroom..." he laughed...

"Harland!" Helen exclaimed...

"Yes Dear?" Judge Duffey said as he took her hand and kissed it...

"Nothing... I love you..."

"I love you too..."

"Aww..." we all said in unison as the waitress and waiter brought our appetizers to the table...

"Damn this looks good – and I'm hungry!" I exclaimed..."

"Me too..." Sheila said...

"Si, si..." Josefina said as we all started passing the plates and helping ourselves...

"More champagne?" the waitress asked...

"Yes please!" Judge Duffey said...

"Yes Please..." Bazil said...

"None for me..." Smalls said...

"I'll have some more..." Sam said...

"Ummm... Sam?"

"Yes Joselyn?"

"Aren't you driving?"

"Nope..." Sam laughed...

"I'll have another..." Troy said...

"No thank you..." Sheila said...

"None for me..." Joselyn said...

"Here!" Keisha said as we laughed...

"Yes, thank you..." I said...

"I'll have some too..." Helen said...

"How was the food?" the waitress asked...

"I hate brussel sprouts – but now that I've tasted yours – I like them..." I said...

"I'll be sure to pass that on..." the waitress said... "How was everything else?"

"Good!" we all said in unison...

"That's great – we'll be back with your food in a lil' bit..." she said as she walked away...

"Oh shit! Troy exclaimed when he saw all the food coming...

"Ooohhh... this all looks so good..." I said...

"Who has the Pot Pies?" the waitress asked...

"We do..." Judge Duffey said...

"Okay – who has the Seafood Paella?"

"Me!" Troy said...

"Who has the mango Salmon?"

"Right here!" Keisha said...

"Who has the Seafood Risotto?"

"Me..." Smalls said...

"Who has the Cajun Grilled Altantic Cod?"

"Ci, ci..." Josefina said...

"Who has the Blackened Swordfish Gorgonzola?"

"That's mine..." Joselyn said...

"Okay – I have two Grilled Center Cut Filet Mignon..."

"Right here..." Bazil said...

"Right here..." Sam said...

"Who has the Prime Steak Frites?"

"I do..." Henley said..."

"Okay – I have two Chicken Francaise..."

"That's for me! I exclaimed..."

"Me too!" Sheila exclaimed...

"Alright! I know you just got your dinner but please feel free to let me know if you want dessert – tonight our dessert is Double Fudge Chocolate Cake..." she said as she walked away...

"Ooohhh.... This looks so good!" Bazil said...

"I'ma 'bout to bust it down!" Troy said... "Right Keisha?"

"Mmmm hmmm..." Keisha said as she ate...

"Oh Honey – this pot pie is delicious..." Helen said...

"Brings back memories..." Judge Duffey said...

"¡Dinos! Tell us!" Josefina said...

"Well..." Helen sighed...

"We had seafood pot pies on our first date..." Judge Duffey said as he took Helen's hand and kissed it...

"Aww..." we all said in unison...

"Is it good Sheila?" I asked...

"Oh yes..." Sheila answered and then she put a piece of chicken in her mouth...

"Damn this shit is good!" Smalls said...

"How's your food Joselyn?" Sheila asked...

"It's delicious..." she sighed...

"You alright Sam?" Bazil asked...

"Oh yea – I'm good!" Sam exclaimed. We finished our food and looked round at each other...

"Who's up for dessert?" Bazil asked...

"I'm always up for dessert..." Judge Duffey said as he smiled at his wife mischievously...

"Harland... what in the world is going on with you?" she asked him...

"It is Valentine's Day..." he answered...

"Yes... it is..."

"Let's get dessert..." Bazil said deliberately... breaking their concentration...

"I don't have room for dessert..." Sheila said...

"Shall I bring the cake?" the waitress asked...

"Yes please..." Bazil answered...

"I don't have room for dessert..." Sheila repeated. When the waitress brought the cake to the table, she changed her mind... "Oh I want some of that!"

"Uh uh – you don't have room for dessert!" Henley said as we all laughed... "I knew when you saw that cake you'd want some..." Henley laughed...

"I feel like singing Happy Birthday..." Keisha laughed...

"I'll leave some plates and the cutter..." the waitress said as she went to get the check..."

"Is she in a hurry?" Joselyn laughed...

"No Joselyn – we're not being rushed – we can stay here as long as we like..." Bazil laughed as he got up, started cutting the cake, and passed down the plates...

"Mmmm... this is good..." Judge Duffey whispered to his wife...

"It's a good thing we don't have to work tomorrow..." Sam said...

"Speak for yourself..." Smalls said...

"You work on Saturdays?" Sam asked...

"I'm an attorney – I work 24-7..."

"Desearía que no trabajaras tan duro ... Te extraño ... I wish you didn't work so hard – I miss you..." Josefina said...

"Sé cómo te sientes Josefina, mi esposo solía trabajar en un tribunal superior, a veces no volvía a casa hasta la medianoche ... I know how you feel Josefina – my husband used to work in a higher court – sometimes he wouldn't come home until midnight…" Helen said…

"That was good…" Keisha said…

"It sure was!" Joselyn and I said in unison and then we all laughed…

"We're ready too…" Judge Duffey said as he stood up and Helen stood up with him…

"Thank you again…" Bazil said…

"You're welcome…"

"Thank you for a lovely evening – it was lovely meeting you all…" Helen said…

"Here…" Judge Duffey said as he handed Bazil $500…

"Oh no…"

"I insist…"

"Yes Your Honor…"

"Good night everybody…" Judge Duffey said as he took his wife by the hand and they left…

"They couldn't wait to leave…" Bazil laughed…

"You peeped them too?" Troy laughed…

"Of course…"

"You ready?" Smalls asked Josefina…

"Listo mi amor … Ready my love…"

"It's just getting' past Sheila's bed time…" Henley said…

"We leavin' with them…" Keisha said…

"You ready Joselyn?"

"I'm ready…"

"Okay – let's go home..." Bazil said as we all got up to leave... "I'll see you all outside..." Bazil said as I grabbed the basket and we went to pay the check. When we got outside, everyone was waiting to give us hugs and kisses... "We love you..." Bazil said...

"Love you too!" Henley, Sheila, Joselyn, Sam, Smalls, and Josefina said in unison before they went to their cars. Keisha and Troy walked hand in hand towards the beach and we followed...

"I wish we could stay here a little while..." Keisha sighed...

"We could, but those nice officers are waiting to remind us that the beach is closed..." Bazil said...

"Aiight – let's go..." Troy said as we started walking to the car...

"How was your dinner?" Mike asked as he opened the door for us...

"It was lovely..." Bazil answered as we all got in...

"I'll get you home..." Mike said as he drove off the beach. We got to Keisha and Troy's house first...

"Good night – love y'all..." Keisha said...

"Love y'all..." Troy said...

"We love you too..." Bazil and I said in unison. When we got to our house, Mike got out and opened the doors for us...

"Thank you Mike..." Bazil said...

"Yes Mike – thank you…" I said…

"You're welcome…" Mike said as he got in the car and drove off…

"Are you ready for your wedding night Mrs. Osgood?"

"Yes Mr. Osgood – I'm ready…" I breathed. Bazil opened the door, pulled me inside to the foyer, closed the door, and kissed me hard…

"Oh damn…" I breathed…

"Don't count on getting any sleep tonight…" he said as he picked me up in his arms and carried me upstairs into the bedroom.

Coffee

"Good morning..." Bazil breathed in my ear as he kissed me awake...

"What time is it?" I moaned as I turned to face him and stretched...

"It's time for us to plan our honeymoon..." he breathed as he kissed me...

"I can't wait..."

"Neither can I..."

"Let's see... I came in Connecticut..."

"I don't understand..."

"I'm counting the places I've had orgasms..." I laughed...

"Oh... I see..." he laughed...

"I came in Connecticut..."

"That's one..." he breathed as he kissed me...

"I came in las Vegas..."

"That's two..." he breathed as he kissed me again...

"I came in New Jersey..."

"New Jersey?"

"On the plane... remember?"

"That's three…" he breathed as he kissed me again…

"I'm gonna cum in Nassau…"

"That's four…" he breathed as he kissed me again, this time putting his tongue in my mouth…

"Mmmm… where will I cum next?" I breathed…

"Well…" he breathed as he kissed me again…

"You could cum in here…"

"I could…"

"Let's go downstairs…"

"Okay…"

"I'll make us coffee…"

"Okay…"

"I'll make breakfast…"

"Okay…"

"You let me know where you wanna cum…"

"Okay…"

"And I'll make you cum…"

"Okay!" I squealed as I jumped up out the bed, threw on my robe, and ran downstairs to the kitchen…

"I guess you really wanna cum…" Bazil laughed…

"I do!"

"Okay, okay!" he laughed… "Le'me make coffee…" he said as he took out everything he needed. I sat there watching him intently as he added the water to the pot...

"You're making a big pot of coffee..."

"I am..."

"Hmmm... I guess I'll have to wait and see..."

"It won't be long..." he said as the pot started brewing...

"Hmmm... maybe I wanna cum on your desk again..." I sighed...

"Okay..." Bazil acknowledged as he took two cups out of the cabinet, put them on the counter, and went over to the refrigerator...

"Oh – is it cold outside? Maybe I can cum in the pool!"

"Okay..." Bazil acknowledged as he made our coffee, put the cups on the table, sat in the chair, opened his robe, and smiled at me mischievously...

"Oh my goodness..." I sighed as I got up and went over to him... "You have a serious issue that needs to be addressed..."

"I do..." he agreed as he took a sip of his coffee...

"As much as I'd love to sit on your dick right now... I'm afraid that won't be enough..."

"You could start by sitting on my dick..." Bazil said as he pulled me closer...

"Wait here – I'll be right back..." I said as I hurried out of the kitchen. When I came back, I had a pillow from the sofa in the library...

"Beautiee... what..."

"Drink your coffee Bazil..." I commanded as I picked up my coffee, took a few sips, dropped the pillow on the floor, got down on my knees in front of him, and took his dick in my mouth...

"Beautiee..." he moaned. I took my time taking his dick in my mouth all the way down his shaft so he could feel the warmth...

"Mmmm hmmmm..." I hummed on his dick and then I took it out my mouth...

"Damn..."

"Drink some more coffee..." I commanded as I picked up my cup, drank some more, and put it back down on the table. I waited for Bazil to drink some more coffee and put his cup down and then I took his dick in my mouth again...

"Beautiee... Shit..." he breathed as he held my head and started fucking my mouth...

"Uh uh..." I said before I took his dick out my mouth again...

"Beautiee..."

"Finish your coffee..." I commanded as I picked up my cup, finished my coffee, and put the cup down on the table. I watched as Bazil picked up his cup and swallowed the rest of his coffee so fast that he spilled some out his mouth...

"Aww... you spilled some..." I sighed and then I took his dick in my mouth again...

"Fuck!" he breathed as he grabbed my head and fucked my mouth... "That's it... Suck it..." he growled as I relaxed my throat and he hit my

tonsils... "I'm Cummmmiiinnngggg.....
Uuuuugggghhhh!" I swallowed and continued
sucking s Bazil played in my hair... "Beautiee..."
he whispered. I took his dick out my mouth and
looked up at him...

'Yes my Thirst Quencher?"

"Come here..." he said as he helped me up
off my knees. Bazil picked up the pillow; I picked
up our cups, and took them over to the counter...

"Beautiee... what are you doing?"

"I'm getting us some more coffee..." I said
as I smiled at him mischievously. Bazil watched
as I made us coffee and brought it back to the
table...

"I think that's my new favorite way to have
coffee..." he breathed...

"I'm glad you enjoyed it..."

"Have you decided how you want to cum?"

"Not yet..."

"Maybe you should cum the way I did..." he
said as he put the pillow on the floor in front of
me and dropped down on his knees... "Finish your
coffee..." he commanded. I picked up my coffee
and gulped it down as quick as I could, stopping
twice because it was hot... "Spread your legs..." he
commanded as he deliberately took his time
finishing his coffee... "Come here..." he breathed
as he pulled me down in the chair, put my legs on
his shoulders, and dove in...

"Baaazzziiilll!" I moaned as I grabbed his
head and started riding his face...

"Yes Beautiee... that's it..."

"Huh... Huh... Huh..." Bazil started thrusting his tongue inside my pussy and put his nose underneath the hood of my clit...

"Bazil... Haaa... Haaa.... Haaa...." Bazil took his tongue out my pussy, put two fingers in my pussy, and began massaging my G-spot as he continued licking, sucking, and slurping... and my legs trembled.... "Bazil... Haaa... Haaa.... Yes... Yes... Yes... Don't stop... I'm cummmiinnng... I'm cummmiinnng... I'm CUMMMIINNNG! AAAGGGGHHH!" Bazil took his fingers out my pussy but continued licking and sucking softly as I clamped my legs around his head...

"Wow..."

"Wow is right..." I breathed...

"You want more..."

"Yesss..."

"I need to eat first..." he said as he took my legs down off his shoulders, stood up, and helped me up...

"You just ate..." I breathed as he pulled me into a kiss...

"I certainly did..." he breathed.

Chapter 21

"Welcome to the British Colonial..." the hostess said as we were escorted into the hotel....

"Thank you..." we both said in unison as we walked into the lobby...

"Oh wow – it's even more beautiful in person..." Bazil breathed...

"It certainly is..." I agreed...

"May I have your name?" the clerk asked when we got up to the counter...

"Bazil & Beautiee Osgood..."

"Bazil Osgood? As in Osgood Publishing?"

"Yes..."

"Can I get a picture with you? Please?"

"Beautiee? Is that okay?" Bazil asked me...

"As long as I can get in the picture with you..." I answered...

"Of course!" she squealed as she ran out from behind the counter and took a selfie with us...

"Thank you so much!"

"You're welcome..." Bazil said...

"Here's your keys – your suite is on the 3rd floor..." she said as she handed Bazil the keys...

"We'll get your bags up to your room for you..." the hostess said as we began walking up the staircase...

"This is fabulous..." Bazil said...

"It sure is..." I agreed. When we got upstairs and got to our room, Bazil opened the door and I started to walk inside but he stopped me...

"Wait here..."

"Okay." I watched as Bazil took the bags into the room and then he came back out into the hallway and picked me up in his arms, carried me into the room, kicked the door closed, and carried me to the bed and laid me down on it...

"You made me a promise..." he said as he got undressed...

"Yes my Thirst Quencher..." I breathed...

"It's time to keep that promise..." he said a she got on the bed, lay beside me, and began undressing me...

"Yes my Thirst Quencher..." Bazil unbuttoned my blouse, unclasped my bra, removed them both, and alternated between my left and right breast swirling his tongue around my nipples... "Bazil..." I moaned...

"I know..." he breathed as he opened my pants and slid them off me along with my panties... "Bazil..." I moaned again as he kissed his way up my body, spreading my legs as he did so, until he reached my mouth and then he eased himself inside me... "Huh... Huh... Huh..." I moaned in his mouth...

"Mmmph... Mmmph... Mmmph..." Bazil was smothering me with his mouth and his tongue as he started fucking me harder...

"Mmmm! Mmmm! Mmmm! Mmmm!"

"Mmmph! Mmmph! Mmmph! Mmmph!"

"Mmmm! Mmmm! Mmmm! Mmmm!"

"Mmmph! Mmmph! Mmmph! Mmmph!" Bazil was fucking me harder now and I was cumming all over his dick as he was cumming inside me...

"Mmmm!"

"Mmmph!"

"Mmmm!"

"Mmmph!"

"Mmmm!"

"Mmmph!"

"Mmmm!"

"Mmmmmmmppphhhh!"

"Mmmmmmmmmmmm!"

"Beautiee..." he breathed...

"Yes... my Thirst Quencher..."

"That was intense..." he breathed...

"It sure was..." I breathed...

"Let's just lay here for a while..."

"Okay..." I breathed as we both fell asleep.

"Mmmm... what time is it?" I yawned...

"It's 7 p.m...."

"I'm hungry..."

"So am I..." he breathed as he kissed me...

"Bazil... I need to eat..."

"So do I..." he breathed as he got on top of me and started kissing his way down my body...

"Bazil..."

"Okay... we'll go eat..." he said and then he kissed me... "But after we eat... I want dessert..." he said as he got up and started getting dressed...

"I love dessert..." I said as I smiled at him mischievously...

"If you don't get dressed... I'm taking you back to bed... and I'm not letting you up until tomorrow morning..."

"Okay, okay!" I laughed as I got dressed... "Where are we going?"

"We're going to the Seafire Steakhouse..." Bazil answered as he took my hand and we left the hotel...

"Welcome to Seafire – what can I get you?" the waitress asked...

"I'll have the Steakhouse Burger..." I answered...

"Would you like that well done?"

"Well done..."

"I'll have the same..." Bazil said...

"I'll be back... she said as she left...

"This is a nice restaurant..." I sighed...

"We can come back if you want..."

"Okay..."

"When we finish our burgers, I want to go to the Aura Night Club..."

"Okay..." I sighed as the waitress put two glasses of water on the table...

"Hmmm... I'm surprised she didn't ask what we wanted to drink..." I said...

"We didn't tell her we wanted anything..." Bazil laughed...

"It's fine – I'll drink water now... and liquor when we get to the nightclub..."

"I like when you get drunk..."

"I like it too... as long as you can carry me..." I laughed...

"Here's your burgers – enjoy!" the waitress said as she left the burgers on the table along with the check...

"I guess she's in a hurry..." Bazil laughed as we ate. When we were finished eating, we went over to the Aura Nightclub, which is located in the Atlantis Hotel, on top of the casino. We walked up the grand staircase and when we got to the top, we saw the sunken glass dance floor and we were in awe...

"Ooohhh – let's go get a drink!" I squealed as I took Bazil's hand and led him to the bar...

"What can I get you?" the bartender asked...

"I'll have a Hurricane!" I squealed...

"And for you sir?"

"I'll have a Nassau Royale..." Bazil answered. We got our drinks and sat at the bar for a while, listening to the music and watching everyone enjoy themselves, and then we got up, started dancing, and spent the rest of the night whining and dry fucking to whatever was playing into the wee hours of the morning.